HOMESTRETCH

Also by Paul Volponi

The Hand You're Dealt

HOMESTRETCH

Paul Volponi

Atheneum Books for Young Readers
New York   London   Toronto   Sydney

ATHENEUM BOOKS FOR YOUNG READERS

An imprint of Simon & Schuster Children's Publishing Division

1230 Avenue of the Americas, New York, New York 10020

ATHENEUM BOOKS FOR YOUNG READERS is a registered trademark of Simon & Schuster, Inc.

For information about special discounts for bulk purchases, please contact Simon & Schuster Special Sales at 1-866-506-1949 or business@simonandschuster.com.

The Simon & Schuster Speakers Bureau can bring authors to your live event. For more information or to book an event, contact the Simon & Schuster Speakers Bureau at 1-866-248-3049 or visit our website at www.simonspeakers.com.

Book design by Mike Rosamilia

The text for this book is set in Adobe Caslon Pro.

Manufactured in the United States of America

10 9 8 7 6 5 4 3 2

Library of Congress Cataloging-in-Publication Data

Volponi, Paul.

Homestretch / Paul Volponi.

p. cm.

Summary: Five months after losing his mother, seventeen-year-old Gas runs away from an abusive father and gets a job working at an Arkansas racetrack, surrounded by the illegal Mexican immigrants he and his father blame for her death.

ISBN 978-1-4169-3987-0

[1. Horse racing—Fiction. 2. Horses—Fiction. 3. Jockeys—Fiction. 4. Prejudices—Fiction. 5. Mexican Americans—Fiction. 6. Fathers and sons—Fiction. 7. Runaways—Fiction. 8. Death—Fiction.] I. Title.

PZ7.V8877Hom 2009 [Fic]—dc22

2008030024

ISBN 978-1-4169-9682-8 (eBook)

This text is dedicated to all the horses bred to race in the sport of kings, which all too often sinks into the sport of knaves.

"Some of us are illegal and others not wanted
Our work contract's out and we have to move on."
—Woody Guthrie

Special thanks to:
Carol Chou
Rosemary Stimola
April Volponi
Eva David
Karen Johnson
Gary Contessa

Chapter One

I'VE ALWAYS BEEN SMALL—the shortest kid in my class, from kindergarten through the end of my junior year in high school.

I never felt any bigger than five foot three inches tall, 105 pounds.

I guess it's in my genes, because my dad's small too. But he's always been stronger than me. And whenever Dad drinks enough whiskey and beer, he acts bigger and meaner.

He started drinking a lot more after Mom died in a traffic accident. A sheriff's deputy blew a stop sign and hit her head-on, chasing some beaner who'd jumped behind the wheel of a stolen car because he didn't want to get deported back to stinking Mexico.

"Just two types who'll work for less money than beaners—

dead folks, and live people with less than a shit's worth of pride," Dad always told me. "That's what keeps salaries here in southwest Texas so low. Those cockroaches will work for next to nothing. And if they ever got exterminated off the face of the earth, folks in these parts would have more, including us."

But after Mom got killed, he wouldn't even say "beaners." He'd just spit on the floor anytime somebody mentioned either them or the cops.

I didn't know who I hated or blamed.

I just wished to God that *one* bean-eating Mexican bastard had stayed where he belonged. Because when he sneaked across the border into Texas, he took more from me than I could ever put into words.

There are plenty of legal ones in my high school. Some of them are all right and never give me any problems. The trouble is you can't tell a *legal* from an *illegal* without an immigration officer or border patrol agent patting them down for their papers.

One time around a lunch table at school, with other kids like me, somebody mentioned how you couldn't tell *them* apart. Off of the top of my head I said, "If it looks like a beaner and talks like a beaner, it probably farts like one too."

For about five minutes, while kids were laughing their asses off, it was the most popular I'd ever been.

I told that same joke to Dad.

He loved it and slapped me on the back.

But Mom overheard it, and she gave me a long speech about other people's feelings.

"Think of the times you came home upset because somebody called you 'shrimp' or 'shorty,'" Mom said. "It wasn't a joke to you, because you knew it wasn't one to them."

About two weeks ago, right in the middle of a huge August heat wave, Dad got laid off from work again. This time from a job he'd had for more than a year at a riding stable. That weekend he was glued to the couch watching TV, with a mountain of beer cans growing at his feet. The first day Dad went out to look for a new job, he came home piss drunk, and I got blamed for the house being a total mess and all the dirty dishes in the sink.

"Animals live in filthy pens! Animals! Not human beings!" he hollered, with his eyes going wild, like they belonged to somebody else—somebody I'm ashamed to say he'd become more than once before.

It had been five months of living hell since Mom was killed.

There wasn't a second in all that time I didn't feel totally ripped apart. Every bit of my life had nose-dived—home, school, friends.

Some small part of me still hoped Dad would step up and be there for me, like Mom used to. But the truth was that he couldn't even take care of himself.

It was mostly on my shoulders.

When I stopped studying last semester, that was all right with Dad because he wasn't sure what grade I was in anymore.

If *I* didn't go to the supermarket, there was no food in the house.

And if *I* didn't do the laundry, we walked around like dirty bums.

"I'll get my own job and you can clean!" I screamed back.

But with nearly every out-of-work high school kid hunting for a summer job too, that hadn't happened yet. And now maybe even Dad, who didn't have a high school diploma, was in line behind some of them.

"So now *you* don't have any respect for me!" he exploded, pulling his belt loose from the loops of his pants. "But you're gonna learn some, *little boy*."

Dad took that leather belt to me, blabbering about money,

bills, and how far he was on the bottom. And he kept calling out Mom's name, "Maria."

I can still hear the *crack* of it against my skin and feel the welts rising up.

The last time he'd smacked me around and then sobered up, he'd promised never to lay another hand on me.

"Gas, I'm sorry. I swear on your mother's grave—may she rest in peace—it'll never happen again. Never," he'd said, with more tears in his eyes than mine.

I believed him.

When Dad passed out cold on the couch with that belt in his hand, I thought about sticking my foot as far up his ass as it could go.

But something inside me felt as sorry for him as I did for myself.

Only, I couldn't let him break his word to me again, or have his lies cost Mom a moment of peace.

She didn't deserve that, and neither did I.

So I emptied out what was left in Dad's wallet.

Then I packed a knapsack and split.

I wasn't about to call the sheriff and have his deputies ride me anywhere in one of those damn squad cars. I hit the side of the highway, walking with my thumb up to hitch a ride.

* * *

"Sure you're not a runaway?" asked an older lady with silver blue hair who took me east. "I don't need any trouble with the law over doing a good deed."

"I just look extra young for my age, ma'am," I answered, showing her the ID I'd doctored to make myself old enough to get a tattoo of a cross with Mom's name on it.

"Gas-ton Gi-am-ban-co Jr.," she read, one syllable at a time. "My, that's quite a mouthful."

"Most everybody I know calls me Gas," I said.

"Well, Gas, you know exactly where you're headin' to, or you gonna find out the closer you get?" she asked.

I hadn't thought about anything like that. I just wanted to get as far away as I could—from everybody and everything around me.

I probably wanted to get as far away as that beaner did after the deputy plowed into Mom's car. And if I ever *could* get there, I'd even things up with that Mexican bastard for sure.

But I didn't have an answer for that lady.

So I shrugged my shoulders to her question. And when I did, I felt the sting across my back where Dad had whipped me.

Two hours later I caught a second ride farther east, from a family in an SUV with two clear-skinned kids around my age.

They were coming back from a Bible meeting, and I even had to mouth a chorus of hymn music when the rest of them joined in with the radio.

Amazing grace, how sweet the sound
That saved a wretch like me
I once was lost, but now am found,
Was blind, but now I see.

"You must be so excited to start college a year early," said the girl, twirling a finger through her curly brown hair. "But having some pickpocket steal your bus ticket. I can't imagine."

"It's sad, but there are all kinds in this world," said the mother.

"All kinds," I echoed, shaking my head.

"Won't your aunt be worried when she meets the bus and you're not on it?" asked the father as his eyes met mine in the rearview mirror.

"Somebody who's getting off at my stop is going to let her know," I answered.

Over the past few months I'd got real good at lying, explaining the reasons for all my bumps and bruises to people.

Slipping down stairs.

Crashing my bike.

Horseback riding accident.

I had a head full of them now, and they popped out of my mouth anytime I needed one.

"Well, we're happy to take you as far as Tyler. That's where we start heading in another direction," the father said.

"That's great," I told him from the extra row of seats in the back they'd pulled down for me. "I can't wait to catch up with my aunt again and settle in over the next couple of weeks before classes start in September."

Half the time I was riding with them, I was watching the oncoming headlights in the opposite lane. I kept waiting for one of those big Mack trucks to come *screeching* across the double line and rip right through us.

And if that happened, I knew in my heart I'd be the only one to walk away. I'd keep heading right on down that highway with every part of me on fire.

The stars had opened their eyes wide by then, and that family dropped me off at a rest stop that had a service station and a bunch of all-night fast-food places.

The son got out of the car with me, clutching his Bible.

"Losing both of your parents in the same year, and still graduating before your class. You've been blessed with great strength, Gas," he said, tapping the book. "I'll pray for you."

He was nearly a foot taller than me, and the glow from the fluorescent lights looked like a halo over his head.

"Thanks," I said, staring straight into his chest. "But I don't deserve it."

Then I walked away, with the biggest part of me wishing I really were an orphan.

A sign read, WELCOME TO TYLER, THE ROSE CAPITAL OF AMERICA.

Only, the night air around *me* smelled of nothing but sweat and car exhaust fumes.

I went into a Burger King and filled my belly with a Double Whopper. I even took one of those cardboard crowns they give away, remembering when I was a little kid how Mom used to pretend with me that our apartment building was a castle.

But there was no use in pretending anymore.

When I finished eating, I parked myself outside on a curb, counting every pockmark on the face of the full moon.

A flatbed truck stacked high with cages of live chickens rolled past me. The air brakes let out a *pssst* as it settled to a stop maybe fifty yards from where I was.

I watched the driver go around back, pulling down cages from the center row.

That's when four shadows hopped off, disappearing into the service station's bathroom.

I had no idea on the walk over what I was going to say to that driver. But I was moving slow, trying to give my brain time to think.

He was leaning against the side of a big tire, smoking a cigarette.

Before I said a word, I heard those shadows jump back onto the truck, with the chickens making noise over it.

"I'm headed north, kid," the driver said, looking at my knapsack. "But this ain't a charity. It'll cost ya."

I fanned out twelve bucks for him to see, knowing I still had some singles and change stuffed down into another pocket.

"You're a small enough package," he said, snatching a pair of five spots. "That'll do."

I thought I'd be riding in the cab with him. But he took me around back and boosted me up onto the flatbed.

"Company's coming, amigos," he called out softly.

I started down a dark three-foot-wide alleyway with feathers and chicken scratch at my feet.

A flashlight shone into my eyes and I squinted to see.

I heard a voice say something low in Spanish, and my insides froze up.

I turned around quick at the sound of the driver putting those cages back into place, barricading me in. And I could see my shadow stretching tall on the floor in front of me.

"Quién es?"

"Un chico pequeño."

Then the flashlight went dead.

I heard the driver's door slam shut and felt the horsepower in that engine rev high.

The truck jolted forward and I nearly fell over.

I locked my fingers around the bars of a cage to keep my balance, when a chicken pecked at them so hard I had to let go.

All I could figure was that I was locked in with a bunch of border-jumping beaners. My legs folded up beneath me and I sank to the floor, with every bit of blood in my veins running cold.

I didn't know who they were or anything about them. I didn't know if they were factory workers, fruit pickers, or criminals. Or if any of them were related to that miserable beaner who'd got Mom killed.

They were just shadows in the darkness. But something inside me wanted to tear them all to pieces. So I pulled off my sweatshirt, down to a white T with the sleeves cut off, showing the tattoo on my right bicep and flexing whatever muscles I had.

Chapter Two

THE STEADY RUMBLING OF the road must have hypnotized me, because I remember opening my eyes with the sun already up.

My legs and rear end had gone almost completely numb. And as I shifted around in that cramped space and the blood started circulating again, a feeling came back into them like I was sitting on needles and pins.

It was the first time I could really see those beaners, and just one of them was awake.

He looked a few years older than me, and he was staring straight at the tattoo on my arm.

"*Mi madre se llama María,*" he said, kissing the fingers on his right hand and then touching them to his heart.

I had to go inside my brain, slowing down what he'd said

and pulling each word apart. But before I got it translated, he said in broken English, "Me—mother name María."

That hit me hard, and I had to fight back a flood of tears.

I guess he noticed, because he backed off and didn't say another word to me. I hated that beaner's sympathy, and I hated him for having a mother with the same name as mine.

After that I didn't want to look at him, and I just stared at those rows of stupid chickens. They were probably on their way to some butcher or slaughterhouse and didn't even know what was coming.

Two more of those beaners woke up and saw the tattoo. And after one of them said my mother's name, that first beaner stopped him cold with a whirlwind of Spanish too fast for me to follow.

That's when I hustled to get my sweatshirt back on.

Only, by then the stench of chicken shit was all over it.

And that smell was probably all over me, too.

Mom always smelled like roses. I don't think it was her perfume, or even the time she spent working at her job in a hothouse raising flowers. It was probably something natural.

"It's only the size of somebody's heart that matters," she'd say whenever I was dragging over being the smallest kid in school. "Look at your father. He's small too. But he's got a big heart."

Dad never laid a hand on Mom or me while she was still alive. But he could lose his temper in a heartbeat, and he'd punched plenty of holes in the plasterboard walls of our apartment when he was sober. He'd been through lots of jobs, like working construction, landscaping, house painting, and roofing. Everything would be going great for maybe six or seven months, and then something would always happen.

He'd get into a fight with his boss or a customer and get himself fired.

Once the sheriff showed up at our front door warning him not to come within five hundred feet of his ex-boss. And every time Dad got canned, he'd have that same excuse ready: "It's easier for them to hire some beaner who'll work for half of what I was making and keep his mouth shut about getting screwed out of overtime, too."

In between jobs one time, when it was just Mom working, Dad was half drunk, sanding the paint off a beat-up kitchen chair.

"Ever feel like you're not good enough, Gas?" he asked as I got home from school. "Like there's a ton of shit out there, and you can't figure out how most of it gets dumped on you?"

Hearing that was like looking into a mirror, and I was too busy staring at myself to answer.

"Your mother's the only one who's ever believed in me. I'd be nothing without her," he said. "But women, they dump little losers like me for somebody better every day. That's the world. That's reality."

"That's not going to happen," I said, feeling like I had to defend her.

"Who knows? Maybe you're right. Her grandparents on both sides are from Spain. They follow tradition there—all about family. I don't care if they speak Spanish the same as shit-hole Mexico. They're nothing like them beaners from across the border," he said. "Anyway, *you* got nothing to worry about. She's your flesh and blood. She can never ditch you."

That was the first time I ever grabbed hold of the idea that he was jealous of my relationship with Mom.

When Dad got that job at the stables, Mom wanted me to learn how to ride. At first I was too scared to get up on a horse. They were so much bigger than me, with a mind of their own.

I guess Mom saw that.

"I haven't done this since I was a little girl," she said, hopping onto a horse that Dad had saddled for me. "Tell me, Gas. You gonna let your old mother show you up?"

That practically *shamed* me into it.

So I pulled up all my nerve, climbing onto the next one.

Dad walked us both around the riding ring.

I'd hardly ever seen Dad like that before. He was calm and in control, and those two big horses acted like they loved him to death. He'd nicker to them softly—*chha, chha*—and they'd just follow him anywhere.

Mom was smiling in the saddle next to me, enjoying every second of it. And after my heart stopped racing, I did too.

I looked down from on top of that horse at everything around me, and it was the tallest I'd ever been in my life.

The flatbed hit a bump, and my eyes landed back on that first beaner. That's when he looked right at me to talk.

"Nacho," I thought I heard him say, tapping his chest.

And I nearly laughed in his face at that.

"Mis hermanos—Anibal y Rafael," he said, pointing to the other two. "Me—brothers."

I just nodded my head with the vibrations of the truck and never even thought about telling him *my* name.

The fourth beaner traveling with those brothers was much older. At first I figured he was their father or uncle. But they never looked at him once like he meant anything to them.

That last beaner was twice as filthy as the other three, with a scruffy beard that the flies from the chickens were nesting in. And when he finally woke up, he started drinking from a small bottle of brown whiskey.

"To Amereeeca 'n' da money!" he hollered, raising his bottle.

Then he started laughing out of control, slapping Nacho's chest for him to celebrate too.

Neither Nacho or his brothers looked happy about it.

I couldn't tell if that beaner was drunk or just plain crazy.

"Los caballos americanos!" he shouted at the top of his lungs. *"Y los caballerizos mexicanos!"*

Except for the "American" and "Mexican" parts, I had no idea what that gibberish meant.

The next time he went to slap at Nacho, the three of them grabbed him hard. The bottle went flying up into the air, bouncing off the top of the truck's cab.

I heard it shatter onto the highway, and the truck driver blasted his horn.

WHOOOOOOO!

The chickens flew into a frenzy, clucking and pecking at one another.

That lunatic beaner was buried at the bottom of the pile

now, with them all cursing in Spanish. And I was worried that one of them might pull out a box cutter or a switchblade.

The driver got off the highway at the next exit, rolling down an incline and stopping at the first light on the service road.

He came around back and pulled down the middle row of cages, waving a Louisville Slugger.

"Let's go, you damn Mexicans!" he screamed, like he'd smash their heads to squash. "We're close enough! Find your own way from here! Out! Out!"

He didn't need to speak any Spanish because that baseball bat was doing all the talking.

I pressed my back up against the cages as they filed past me, jumping off the truck.

"You too! You're no better than *them*!" the driver yelled at me.

Hearing that was nearly the same as getting smacked in the mouth with that bat.

I wanted to tell that driver how I was just like *him* and should have been riding up front in the cab all along. I wanted to beg him to leave me off anywhere else in the world except next to those beaners.

But he was as angry as Dad at his worst, without even drinking. And I didn't want to risk hearing what else he might say.

He drove off, leaving us stranded on the corner of Lost and Nowhere, sandwiched between the highway overpass, a fenced-off soccer field, and a little park with picnic tables at the very beginning of some neighborhood of identical single-family houses.

Those stupid beaners stood there arguing with one another.

The spit was flying everywhere, until the one who'd been drinking raised his middle finger to the rest of them and *me*.

"*Putos grandes!*" he sneered, bringing his hands apart wide.

Then he left. I watched him stagger away, crisscrossing the solid yellow lines in the street back toward the overpass.

Right then I couldn't have cared less if some sheriff's deputy came speeding from the opposite direction with his lights flashing and siren blasting, flattening his ass into Mexican roadkill.

The sun was blazing hot, so I headed for a tree and some shade inside that park.

Nacho and his brothers were busy at a corner pay phone, before they came over to where I was.

"Change, *por favor?*" Anibal asked, with the others nudging him forward. "Please, *señor*. Change?"

Those beaners didn't even have a dollar bill to trade. They were looking for a handout, and that pissed me off beyond belief.

I dug deep into my front pocket, then flung a fistful of dimes and nickels at them.

"Here, fuckos!" I shouted. "Like I'm not broke enough for you!"

Then I watched them pick through the grass and dirt for every last one. And everything Dad had ever said about them taking *our* jobs and *our* money echoed inside my head.

I was trying to make a plan for myself when Nacho came running back, with his brothers still on the phone.

"*Dónde?* Where is—here?" he asked, out of breath.

That's when it hit me for real that *I* had no idea where I was.

So I just stared at him cold and blank, without even blinking.

Rafael went up to a car at a red light and must have got the answer, because he sprinted back to Anibal, who was holding the phone, telling him something.

For the next three or four hours I sat underneath that tree drawing in the dirt with a stick, wondering if Dad knew I was gone yet, or if he even cared. Nacho and his brothers spent most of that time staring down the service road, like some magic carpet for beaners was about to come sailing through.

Only, I was wishing it would be the dogcatcher instead.

The cars that drove past mostly had Lone Star State license plates. But I was seeing more and more cars with Arkansas, Oklahoma, and Louisiana tags too. So I figured I was close to the northeastern tip of Texas, where all those states practically met. But it bothered me bad that those beaners probably knew exactly where we were and I didn't.

I wasn't about to ask *them* or anybody else.

It was closing in on dinnertime and I was still stranded in that park, twenty yards from Nacho and his brothers, like there was an invisible string tied between us.

My stomach was grumbling, so I broke down and bought myself an ice cream sundae and a soda off a white truck with jingling bells. That left me with just three lousy bucks to my name. But I enjoyed every bit of that food in front of those starving beaners, who'd been sucking water from a fountain and eating shriveled figs off a tree.

A few joggers showed up, along with some parents bringing their young kids to the park's playground after work.

Most of them were staring at us.

"For Christ's sake! You all gonna pitch a tent and live here?" barked a man walking a big German shepherd. "This ain't a refugee camp!"

I knew it was a matter of time before somebody called the cops.

Then, just as the sun was sinking low, a rusted horse trailer pulled up to the curb, and those beaners shot up at attention like they'd been drafted into the Mexican army.

The man who got out was tall, and as thin as a whip, leaning off to one side. He had on mirrored sunglasses, with a toothpick rolling around in his mouth, and there was a small alligator over his shirt pocket.

"There's supposed to be *four* of you!" he yelled. "*Four!* Can't you fucking count, muchachos?"

Nacho called out to me in a panicked voice, "Come! *Trabajo!* Work—money!"

I didn't know what *work* those beaners had waiting—the kind that was worth crossing the border and riding all this way surrounded by stinking chickens. But it was probably better than what was waiting for me if I had to go crawling back home, or if the cops dragged me there.

Besides, I was going to need money to survive, to put a roof over my head. And just like Dad, I was unemployed.

So I walked over and let that man grill me up and down through those mirrored glasses, like I was a week-old burrito at a 7-Eleven he was thinking about stomaching.

I just stood in front of him with my mouth shut tight.

When he finally nodded his chin, I climbed into the back of that empty horse trailer behind Nacho and his brothers. It was almost pitch-black in there, and I stood up the entire ride, with my eyes peering out between the wooden slats of a window.

I needed to see every sign along the highway and know *exactly* where I was.

Chapter Three

WE ROCKETED UP INTERSTATE 30 past Texarkana, with that whip of a man hitting the horn and riding up on the bumper of every car that didn't move out of his way fast enough.

I stood at the window the whole time, with those Mexican jumping beans sitting at my feet, bouncing around at every bump.

Right before we hit Hot Springs, Arkansas, that man got off the highway and snaked down the side roads about a mile.

The huge sign over a high chain-link fence read, PENNINGTON RACETRACK.

There was a painting of a racehorse with its jockey on that sign. And I guess the dark lines sweeping straight back off the two of them were supposed to make you believe how fast they were going.

We passed through the racetrack's gates, and the driver

stopped in front of a security station. Then he hustled us out of the trailer into a small brick building where a fat sergeant sat behind a desk with his feet up, watching *America's Funniest Home Videos*.

"Newbies? This time of night, Dag?" the sergeant asked him, annoyed.

I didn't know what kind of name Dag was, but the more I watched the sharp point of that toothpick rolling around in his mouth, the more it seemed to fit him.

"Emergency—had a whole family of Mex grooms quit me for a track in Oklahoma," Dag answered, slipping him a twenty. "I had to go pick these boys up myself. So just *express* them for me. Will ya?"

The sergeant handed each of us a yellow card to fill out and pointed to the lines on them with a stubby finger.

"Name—here. Birth date—here," he said slow and steady, like we were retards.

Then Dag took the cards to write his name in the space that read "Employer."

I looked up at the TV to see some father lob a baseball to his little son, who was waiting there with a bat on his shoulder. The kid smacked a line drive right back into his father's nut sack.

The sergeant howled over that, and so did I.

But those beaners never smiled, and just winced at the replay.

"GAS-TON GI-AM-BANC-O!" Dag roared after reading my card. "WHAT THE HELL'S THIS?"

"That's me," I answered. "It's my name."

"You're not a groom from Mexico?" he asked, with the sergeant laughing more at Dag now than that TV show.

"I know lots about horses. Really. My dad worked at a riding stable," I answered.

"Oh, did he. Well, la-di-fucking-da." Dag smirked. "Do you know the family of *these* boys have groomed racehorses for generations? That their father's father's father probably came to this country to take care of horses? It's in their blood. It's what they dream about. Your *dad* worked at a riding stable. Doing what—shoveling horse shit?"

I saw my reflection in his mirrored glasses, and I never looked so small.

"*Boy*, you're lucky I need a hot walker," Dag said, crossing out one of the lines on my card and writing in something new. "But they make a hundred and forty dollars less a week than grooms do. So live with it."

I didn't even know what a hot walker did.

I'd seen a guy walk barefoot over hot coals once at a carnival. Dad swore the guy had probably made some kind of deal with the devil to do it. But I never believed that.

Anyway, I had a job now.

A hundred and forty less a week meant I'd be getting paid something, even if it wasn't as much as those beaners.

I knew I was twice as smart as them and would probably be their boss inside of a week.

The sergeant took Polaroids of us. Then he pasted our pictures on those ID cards, and I saw white spots in front of my eyes from the flash of that camera for close to five minutes.

"These cards—*muy im-por-tante*. Wear them all the time—on your outside clothes," the sergeant said, tugging at the tin badge pinned to his shirt. "With them you're *legal* on the racetrack. Without them you're an *illegal*. Understand?"

Nacho and his brothers nodded their heads in excitement, like they'd just been made U.S. citizens.

I looked at my card and saw that Dag had changed my date of birth. I wasn't thinking and had put down my real one.

On the walk out Dag asked me, "What's your name again, kid?"

"Gas," I answered, cautious.

"Well, genius Gas, you need to be eighteen to live and work on the racetrack. Remember that."

At the time I believed he was doing *me* the favor.

Dag drove us to his barn on the racetrack's backstretch—

where the rows of stables, the dorms, and the cantina were. But it was closing in on ten o'clock that night, and most everything there was stone quiet.

The sign on the side of his cinder-block barn read in big black letters, DAMON DAGGET—PUBLIC RACING STABLE.

The horses whinnied loud—*whhhaaa*—at the sound of his trailer pulling up.

Then Dag cut the engine and everything fell silent again.

We ducked under a waist-high wooden latch, following Dag inside his barn, past the night watchman. There was a long row of fourteen stalls, with a powerful Thoroughbred standing tall in each one. There were another fourteen horses in the stalls behind them, and a curve on each end of the barn, which was laid out in a tight oval.

"This way—*venga*," said Dag, showing Nacho and his brothers the horses they'd be grooming.

Each of them got two Thoroughbreds to take care of.

"Ah, sí," those beaners said, back and forth. *"Bueno."*

They walked up to the stall doors, kissing and stroking their horses on the nose, looking them over from head to toe. I would have sworn those stupid beaners were in love. But if it had been up to me, I wouldn't have given them a jackass to look after in this country.

I glanced over Nacho's shoulder as he moved to the next stall. The gold nameplate on the leather-strapped halter around that horse's head and powerful jaw read, BAD BOY RISING.

There was fire in that horse's eyes and a long blaze of white hairs running down his dark brown face. Something made me reach out to pet him, and Bad Boy Rising tried to take a vicious bite out of my hand.

"If that one had as much speed as he does attitude, he wouldn't be one step away from the slaughterhouse. From the stable to the dinner table, that's what's waiting for this one if he don't win soon," said Dag. "As for you, *you'll* be walking horses in circles after they come back from training every morning. You'll pick 'em up hot and walk till they've cooled down. Forty minutes each you'll walk 'em. Then we'll see how much *gas* you got in your tank."

Dag said it was too late that night to get registered for a dorm room. So he walked us past his office, which had a comfy-looking leather sofa and chairs, and into a stuffy equipment room without windows that was maybe half the size. It was filled with dusty horse blankets, bridles, whips, riding helmets, and worn-out saddles.

"They'll all sleep in here tonight," Dag told the night watchman, who had some Spanish in him. "I'm heading home for some shut-eye."

Then Dag's wiry frame dipped under the wooden latch and he was gone.

That night the four of us slept shoulder-to-shoulder on the dirt floor, under horse blankets. And before the light got turned out, I looked at the yellow ID card hanging over Nacho's heart and saw that his name was really Ignacio.

From near the end of my sophomore year until the week before she died, Mom drove me down to the stables on Fridays, just before Dad knocked off work.

In the beginning I was happy with my horse just walking the trail—its nose following the tail of the one in front of it. But Mom kept pushing me to gallop with her.

"Come on, Gas. You wanna feel those four legs flying beneath you," she'd say. "Think about the poor horse. He was born to run, not be bored out of his mind playing follow the leader in slow motion."

Only, I wouldn't budge.

Then one day Dad sneaked up from behind, without Mom seeing, and whispered to me, "Hold on tight."

He slapped my horse hard on the backside.

That horse took off running and I lost my balance.

I had both arms locked tight around its long neck, fighting

to hang on. I could hear Mom's horse chasing after me, and her yelling, "Pull on the reins!"

But I couldn't. And after fifty or sixty yards I lost my grip, tumbling to the gravel-covered ground.

Once Mom saw I was all right, she rode past me, running down the loose horse. Dad walked over to where I was, and his boss came charging out of the office.

"This isn't some damn rodeo! What's goin' on here?" he hollered, staring Dad down.

Dad cleared his throat, kicking away the rocks at his feet.

Before he said a word, I answered, "It's *my* fault, sir. I got a big head, thinking I could really ride. That's all."

I took the blame because I didn't want Dad to get into any kind of argument and maybe get fired again. Mom was so happy with him working there, and I figured he was better off around those horses than spreading hot tar across somebody's roof.

Mom brought the horse back by the bridle, and Dad checked him over.

"No worse for the wear," he told his boss.

"Gas, I fell plenty of times. You just gotta climb right back on," Mom said. "It's the only way."

"She's right," echoed Dad. "Let's go."

Then he cupped his hand and gave me a boost into the saddle.

"More important, you gotta learn to listen, son," Dad said harsh, before he apologized to his boss for what *I'd* done.

That really got me pissed. Dad made it sound like he'd warned me a hundred times. And maybe even *he* believed it was my fault now.

Dad never thanked me for taking the heat. He never even mentioned it, and Mom never found out what really happened.

By the next week I was hell-bent on galloping that same horse, just to show up Dad. And I did.

It was like flying on the wind, and it made me forget for a while about how being so small had me weighed down.

I hadn't been on a horse in five months now.

Not since Mom was killed.

I got woken up that next morning just after five o'clock, when the beaners who worked at Dag's barn came into the equipment room and saw Nacho and his brothers. They all began hugging one another and *"mi familia"* was on nearly everyone's lips as they moved around me like I was invisible.

That's when I realized *all* of Dag's workers, except for me, were Mexican.

They all started pulling out the horses' feed tubs and

hayracks. I stumbled around lost in that mix for more than a half hour. Then I spotted a big copper pot by Dag's office and spooned myself some oatmeal.

Dag was busy inside on the phone. But some heavyweight beaner was barking out orders at everyone in Spanish.

"Breakfast finished," he snapped through a thick accent, pushing a rake into my hands. "You clean up outside. Horses ready to walk later."

It didn't take me long to figure out that he was Dag's assistant, and what Dad always called the HMIC—Head Mexican in Charge.

Then I heard somebody call him Paolo, before he snapped at me a second time, "Go work, *gringo!*"

I squeezed the rake tight, and in my bones I knew that except for Nacho, Rafael, and Anibal—who'd just got to this country—any of those beaners could have been the one who got Mom killed.

That burned inside of me, and I wondered how much you could hate somebody you'd never seen, just hating the idea of *him*. Hating that he was still alive, and breathing the air in this country he didn't deserve.

The sky was still dark and I could barely see the ground outside. But I kept scratching at it with that rake, harder and harder, wanting to dig my way to China, or Spain, where Mom's *familia* was from.

A beaner came flying up to the barn on a bike, pedaling his ass off. He must have been really late, because he ditched the bike in the grass with the front wheel still spinning.

I was probably just a shadow to him as he bolted past, touching me on the shoulder.

"Buenos días," he said, disappearing into Dag's barn.

I hadn't washed in two days, so I didn't know who or what I smelled like anymore. The salt from my sweat was stinging my eyes, and I felt like I'd just crawled out of some hole.

A beaner had just mistaken me for one of his own.

That's when I knew I couldn't sink any lower.

I stood there like a statue, leaning on that rake with my emotions frozen solid.

Then slowly the darkness started to fade.

I heard a cock crow—*ererEREEEERRrrrr.*

A warm glow found the back of my neck, and I turned around.

The sun was coming up over the huge, empty grandstand, and the rays of light were reflecting off the small lake in the middle of the racetrack's infield.

The growl of engines was growing louder, heading in my direction.

So I walked down a grassy hill, maybe twenty yards.

I put both hands on the white rail and stared down the straightaway of racetrack.

A tractor came rolling past, dragging a heavy metal claw with long iron fingers that turned over the dirt, making it an even darker brown.

Then a truck came behind that, spraying a mist of water.

My lungs were breathing it all in deep, like I'd been suffocating for a long time without knowing.

Suddenly, the rhythm of hoofbeats drummed along the racetrack.

Through the sun's glare I could see the silhouette of a woman galloping a horse. I closed my eyes and listened—*brrmp-brrmp-brrmp-brrmp*—as she rode past.

For a few seconds everything I'd been holding back inside of me melted down. I wish I could have stopped time right there, in that paradise. I wanted to plant my feet into the ground and never move again, like a tree with roots.

Chapter Four

THE FIRST OF DAG's horses to come back from training at the racetrack that morning was Bad Boy Rising. Nacho stood him outside in the sun on a pair of black rubber mats laid side by side. Then he handed me the leather lead shank. It was like holding a huge dog on a leash—one that was a foot and a half taller than me and outweighed me by more than a thousand pounds.

Bad Boy shook his head from side to side, eyeing me like he could take off anytime he wanted, and my whole body began to quiver.

But Nacho chirped to him and turned the hose on a soapy sponge inside of a silver bucket. Then he started to scrub away at Bad Boy Rising's neck, and I could feel that horse begin to relax.

When the bath was over, I started walking Bad Boy Rising in circles around the barn to dry off and cool down his muscles.

He was tugging hard the whole way, testing me. And I had to use all my strength to keep him going in a straight line.

"Bad Boy say he's the boss of you, too!" boomed Paolo for half the barn to hear. "He show everybody how far down you are!"

Hardly any of those beaners needed *that* translated, because most of them were laughing along with Paolo.

On my last lap around the barn with Bad Boy Rising, I saw a saddle sitting on the stall door of one of Rafael's horses. It was black with a picture of a red, pointy-tailed devil holding a fiery pitchfork stitched into the side. A dark-skinned exercise rider who was talking to Dag saw me looking at it. He stopped in midsentence and stared laser beams through me, like he'd whip my ass from here to tomorrow for having my eyes on his saddle.

He was no bigger than I was and probably as old as my dad.

But his hot glare nearly turned my legs to butter. So I dropped my eyes to the floor fast and kept walking while I still could.

When I circled back around, Rafael had just finished tightening the black saddle on his horse. Dag gave a leg up to that devil rider, who clenched the whip between his teeth as he tightened the reins with both hands. Then he took the horse down to the track, with Dag slithering alongside. And I started to breathe a lot easier with him gone.

I'd walked three more horses around the barn that morning before I noticed another hot walker taking one into an open courtyard between a half dozen different stables. That courtyard had a narrow dirt path circling a huge shade tree, where horses were walking single file.

When Nacho finished giving his other horse a bath, I took the bucket of soapy water and poured it over my head.

Nacho smiled, sniffing at his sweat-stained armpits, and said, "May-be I need."

"*Sí*. Every day from now on," I sniped, squeezing my nostrils shut between two fingers and wondering if beaners even had soap in their stinking country.

I took Nacho's horse, an easygoing filly named Rose of Sharon, out to that courtyard, looking for a change of scenery. I'd been walking her for maybe five minutes when that devil rider brought another runner of Dag's back to the barn. I tried to ignore him, but my eyes met his anyway, like some kind of magnetic force was pulling them into line.

Then he stood in the saddle, hocking up a wad of phlegm from his throat and spitting into the grass as he rode past.

"So you just got here, and El Diablo thinks you're clam juice," said a soft voice from behind me. "Well, all right for you."

I turned to see who it was, and it was like getting hit by a lightning bolt—she was that beautiful.

Her silky blond hair was bouncing off to the side in a ponytail. There was a silver cross on a chain lying flat against her chest, and the loose white blouse she had on reminded me of an angel's robes. She was an eyelash taller than me—not too short for a girl—and probably a year or two older than I was pretending to be.

I stopped in my tracks and struggled hard to find my tongue as she kept her horse a good ten feet in back of mine.

"All I did was look at him," I finally said.

"That'll do it," she said, jutting out her chin as a signal for me to keep walking my filly.

"Why do they call him that?" I asked, moving forward, even though every thought in my mind was on her.

"Comes from his days riding in Peru, when his horse trampled another jockey during a race and killed him, his own brother," she said. "Then he came to the States. Trainers say he's so strong that when he whips horses, they run like the devil was chasing them. But two years ago he got caught fixing a race—holding his horse back so a long shot could win and he could cash a bet."

That's when I noticed an old man with his feet planted at the far edge of that circular path.

"At least it's better than doping a horse to run faster than it really can," the old man said to me. "That's what your new boss, Dag, does. Did you know that? One day they'll start testing at Pennington for those magic milk shakes he feeds some of them, and *he'll* be gone."

I wasn't sure what to say back to him, or what a "magic milk shake" was. But I didn't want to make any more enemies, so I answered, "I guess," and followed the circle.

"That's my grandpa, Cap Daly. I work for him," she said as we started back around. "He's been training racehorses here for more than forty years. And in case you haven't figured it out, he hates Dag."

"You think Dag's a crook?"

"Think? I know it," she answered.

"And El Diablo, he did time in prison for fixing races?" I asked, glancing over my shoulder to steal another peek at her.

"Nah. He got probation. Racing commission took his jockey's license and gave him a big fine. All he's allowed to do now is exercise horses. I hear he puts in the paperwork every year, praying to get reinstated. They took away what he loves most—race riding. That's why he's such hell to be around. And in the mornings, out on the racetrack, he's even worse. I won't get anywhere near him when I'm on a horse."

"You're an exercise rider too?"

"I got lots of jobs at the barn. My grandpa can't afford to hire much help these days. He runs a small stable now. Down to just four horses."

"Because of his age?"

"*No,*" she answered short as we made the curve and approached the old man again.

"This one's walked enough, Tammie," said Cap, tipping back his Kangol hat and wiping his forehead dry.

Tammie swung her horse around mine, and I stopped.

"So, Rose of Sharon, who's your friend?" Tammie asked my filly, before she turned her eyes back to me. "She used to be in my grandpa's barn before her owner moved her to Dag's."

"Oh. My name's Gas," I said.

"Really?" she asked. "Because you ride a racehorse so fast?"

I just nodded my head, staring into her honey brown eyes.

Then Cap said, "Gas, I'll give you some good advice. It's for the benefit of *you* and this *filly,* not your boss. You can't turn a horse on tight angles like you been doing. It puts too much pressure on their ankles."

"Thanks," I said. "Forty years, huh? I guess you know everything about training horses."

"I'll know more when they learn to talk," he said, half serious.

"Maybe I'll see you on the racetrack or at the cantina," Tammie called back to me as they walked off.

I turned my head all the way around to keep watching Tammie from behind, as me and Rose of Sharon made the curve for another lap.

By eleven thirty all the horses were back in their stalls eating up, and there wasn't a pile of shit you could see left anywhere in Dag's barn. Just before we quit for the day, Dag called Nacho, Rafael, Anibal, and me into his office.

He was coiled in a leather chair, with Paolo standing next to him.

"*Muchachos,*" Dag said, waving us inside. "Good day's work. *Bueno. Bueno.*"

There was a brown and white chicken on the floor, and Dag had some corn feed in his hand.

"Watch," Paolo told us, pointing to the chicken at Dag's feet.

Dag took off his mirrored glasses, looking that chicken

in the eye. He held his hand over its head, and Paolo put his fingers in front of his mouth, playing an imaginary flute.

"Dee-de-dee-de-de. Dee-de-dee-de-dee-de-de," sang Paolo, like Dag was one of those Arabian snake charmers.

The chicken started walking backward in circles, following Dag's hand like it was hypnotized.

Those beaners were laughing hysterical over that show, and even Paolo, who'd probably seen it lots of times before, stopped singing to slap his sides. But it was all I could do to fake a smile, thinking how I never wanted to become like that chicken, and about what Tammie and her grandpa had said about Dag.

Dag looked at me hard with his dark green eyes.

"I thought you just trained horses," I said, almost in self-defense.

"Plenty of animals in these stables," he answered, putting his glasses back on. "Chickens, dogs, a goat or two. They all help keep the horses calm."

Then Dag stood up and pulled out a roll of bills from the front pocket of his denims. He gave us each forty bucks and said, "Here's an advance on your first week's pay, so you can eat and stuff."

Paolo was translating that into Spanish before the words were out of Dag's mouth.

Nacho and his brothers shook Dag's hand, saying, *"Gracias, Señor Dag. Muchas gracias."*

I was pretty thankful too as his hand clamped around mine.

Then Dag took a fresh toothpick from a little glass cup on his desk. As he started to pick at his teeth, he told Paolo, "Go get these boys settled in right."

Paolo walked us over to the men's dorms, where lots of the workers from the different stables lived.

It wasn't just the workers at Dag's barn who were beaners. Nearly every groom and hot walker I'd seen on the backstretch was Mexican. And it was the same with everybody I saw going in and out of that dorm's lobby.

A list of rules was printed on the lobby wall in Spanish and English.

NO MUJERES. NO NIÑOS.
NO VIOLENCIA.

NO ALCOHOL. NO NARCÓTICOS.

NO WOMEN. NO CHILDREN.
NO VIOLENCE.

NO ALCOHOL. NO DRUGS.

The backstretch dorms were rent-free and built right next to the barns so the workers could be close to the horses in case there was ever an emergency.

The man in charge of the dorms said that only two people were allowed to a room.

"No exceptions. No how. No way," the man went on, with a Southern twang. "I've split up more Mexican families than the U.S. Border Patrol."

That's when Paolo grinned at me, snorting, "Now, who's gonna want to be roommate with *you*?"

I wished I could tell him exactly how I felt. How I'd rather sleep in the monkey house at the zoo, or underneath a pile of garbage at the city dump, than room with a beaner. But I couldn't. I was stuck.

The three brothers looked at one another for a few seconds.

Then Nacho said, "Me. I—go with Gas."

"*Con el gringo,*" howled Paolo.

"*Es un hijo de María,*" Nacho said, pointing to the bottom half of the tattoo beneath my short sleeve. "*Nuestros madre se llama María también.*"

"*Sí. Sí,*" said Rafael and Anibal.

I wanted to punch Paolo in his fat face, but I couldn't afford to get fired. And right then I began to understand how Dad must have felt at some of those jobs he'd had.

Through that whole scene I had one eye glued to the pay phone hanging on the wall. I was thinking about Dad, wondering if he was sober.

I'd been gone nearly two days. I thought about calling. But I was scared to hear his voice. To hear what it would sound like with him knowing I'd ditched him, my own flesh and blood— even though he deserved it.

But I'd have been even more scared to hear that phone keep on ringing, with no one picking up. No answering machine. Nothing.

And I was convinced that if there was no answer, it wouldn't be because Dad was running all over town trying to find me.

Before he left, Paolo slapped me on the back and mocked, "*Gringo*, say hello to your new *familia*. These are your long-lost Mexican brothers."

Chapter Five

I'D JUST GOT HOME from school when a sheriff's deputy banged on our door. At first I figured it was because Dad had lost his temper again, getting into another fight at work. Only, it wasn't.

"Does a female Caucasian here drive a red Honda?" the deputy asked.

"My mom, Maria Giambanco," I answered low.

He said there'd been a traffic accident but wouldn't tell me anything more about it.

"We need an adult to go to the hospital," he said.

I was trembling in the backseat of the squad car, thinking Mom was in surgery or a coma, as that deputy drove me down to the riding stables.

Dad was outside brushing the saddle marks off a horse

when the deputy jumped out. All the windows of the car were shut tight, and I watched their mouths move until Dad hustled that horse inside the barn.

When Dad came back out, he got into the front seat, next to the deputy, instead of sitting with me.

"She'll be okay, Gas. You'll see," he said in a strained voice as I sat alone, behind the steel screen that separated the cops from the criminals.

"There was an illegal behind the wheel of a stolen car, and an officer in another car was involved as well," said the deputy. "I just know that it's serious."

"Damn these bastards!" exploded Dad, punching the dashboard so hard I was scared the air bag was going to fire off.

A cold shiver shot up my spine, and I wished for anything that Dad knew how to hold me. It wouldn't have mattered anyway, because I could barely squeeze my fingertips through the openings in that cold metal screen between us.

The deputy hit the siren, and the sound of it pounded at my eardrums. Then that squad car picked up more and more speed, and everything around me became a blur.

At the hospital Dad found out before I did that Mom had died.

But when I saw Dad's face, he didn't have to say a word to me.

I knew by his blank stare that she was gone, and I sank down deeper into the cushion of the waiting-room chair, never wanting to get up again.

Then Dad went berserk after he saw some beaner in a white uniform cleaning the hospital floor.

"You lousy bastard! You and all your kind!" he screamed, kicking over that beaner's water bucket and chasing him with the mop.

I ran out of that hospital while the deputies were wrestling Dad down. I felt homeless, like I had no one left and nowhere to go.

I walked alone along the side of the highway, crying my eyes out, with the cars roaring past.

Vrrrm. . . . Vrrrm. . . . Vrrrm. . . . Vrrrm. . . .

And it felt like getting socked in the gut a thousand times over.

Our dorm room was basically four walls and two single beds. There was a nightstand with a reading lamp, and in the top drawer there was a Bible, like in a motel. Only that *Biblia* was written in Spanish.

I grabbed the bed closest to the window, cracking it open so I could breathe some fresh air.

On the wall next to me was the Scotch-tape outline of a picture that used to be there. It was important enough to the beaner who'd slept there before me to take it with him. Maybe it was of his *familia*, the horse he groomed, or some gorgeous angel like Tammie. All I know is that empty square kept staring back at me and wouldn't quit.

I blinked first and turned away from it.

"Look," said Nacho, pulling out a plastic see-through container from underneath his bed. And I saw that there was one under mine, too.

There wasn't a dresser or closet in the room, so that was where you were supposed to keep all your stuff. As we both unpacked, it started to sink into my brain. I'd been in this country my whole life, seventeen years. I figured it had been just a couple of days or so since Nacho crossed the border into the United States. Only, now we both wore the same yellow ID card. And he had as much as I did—some underwear, shirts, pants, and a better job to boot.

"Mi madre," said Nacho, showing me a tiny picture from his pocket.

I didn't want to see it. But I didn't want to insult him over his mother, either.

I held it gently by the lower right corner, afraid I'd bend it.

Then I brought it up close to my face.

She had the same straight black hair and cocoa-colored skin as Nacho and his brothers. Her eyes were big and bright, and she smiled, raising the muscles in her cheeks, without opening her lips.

"Beau-ti-ful," I said, handing it back. "She's in Mexico?"

"*Ah, sí,*" he answered. "*Mi padre en California*—at racetrack, groom horses. One day me, *mis hermanos, mi madre*—all go to California."

That's when I realized that Nacho had *a lot* more than me.

There was just one bathroom to a floor, and that was in the hallway. So I had to wait in line behind a parade of beaners to take a shower. When I finally got inside, I eyed that shower stall up and down, checking for cooties. I didn't have my own bar of soap. One was sitting in a soap dish, all lathered up. But I passed on the idea of using it and decided steaming hot water would work good enough.

For dinner I had a Snickers, a 3 Musketeers, and two cans of Dr Pepper from the vending machine in the dorm. Even with all that sugar pumping through me, I was exhausted and slept for almost twelve hours.

The next morning, before the sun came up, I was back working at Dag's barn.

I walked horses in circles for hours, with no sight of Tammie in that courtyard.

El Diablo passed a couple of times without giving me a second look. He was probably busy pressing somebody else that day for no good reason.

Just when I thought my work was done, Dag pointed me toward two huge buckets of shit.

"Haul those over to the manure pits, about a quarter mile up the road. Bet your daddy at the *riding stable* never saw that much manure. It's high quality, too. That's Thoroughbred shit," he said, grinning. "Couple days of workin' for me and you're probably twice the horseman he is."

I was going to say something back, but I didn't want to talk about Dad anymore and have something I didn't want anyone to hear slip out.

The buckets were so heavy I had to make two trips, balancing each one on my shoulder. I was praying I wouldn't run into Tammie right then. And even after I was finished, the stink seemed to hang in the air around me for a while, not wanting to leave.

Before I left, I noticed Rose of Sharon's feed bucket hadn't been filled, and there was webbing up in front of her stall so she couldn't reach her hayrack.

"She race today," said Nacho when he saw me looking. "No full belly. Run faster. *Muy rápida hoy.*"

I was starving for a real meal to fill my own stomach, and started over to the cantina, where I'd seen a food truck parked outside.

The guy who drove it was American, but all the food he had was beaner slop.

His truck was loaded up with tacos, burritos, and enchiladas.

"Don't you have any hamburgers?" I asked him.

"Yeah, at *my* house," he laughed, clicking the silver coin holder on his belt to give some beaner change. "Exactly who would I sell that to here?"

So I passed.

There were forty or fifty bikes leaning up against the cantina, and the sound of Mexican music, filled with wooden guitars and accordions, was pulsing through the walls.

I opened the door and felt like I needed a passport to step inside.

Beaners were crowded around the Ping-Pong and pool tables, watching and waiting their turn. The two big-screen

TVs were both tuned to Spanish stations. One was showing the news, and the other, some kind of soap opera with a slinky *chiquita* in a low-cut dress.

The food counter inside had the same crap to eat as that truck. I went around the whole place twice before I decided I'd walked in enough circles that morning. And as I left, I watched that little white Ping-Pong ball fly over the net as fast as I'd ever seen it, picking up the same rhythm off those paddles as the music that was playing.

Outside, the guy at the food truck pointed over to the tall grandstand and said, "Hey, kid. Try the track. There's racing this afternoon. They've got what you're lookin' for."

He was right.

It was like a carnival over there, with barkers in front of the main gate hawking five-dollar tip sheets that promised to pick you the winner of every race.

I could smell the charcoal burning and the burgers sizzling on a grill inside.

The man at the turnstile saw my yellow ID and waved me in for free.

The front side of the racetrack was filled with *regular* people.

There were old folks sitting in lawn chairs with coolers

at their feet. Teenagers were tossing a football. A guy was walking with his arm around his girl, and her hand was stuffed down into the back pocket of his jeans. There were a bunch of hard hats with their sleeves cut off drinking beers, cursing and slapping at each other for fun. And there were long betting lines everywhere, jammed front to back with people holding money in their fists, ready to pick a horse.

Every Mexican face I saw was either behind a stand serving food or taking tickets. It was like the world I'd always known had been turned right side up again.

"Double fries with the two cheeseburgers, mister?" asked the beaner who served me.

"That's what I like to hear, *Pee-dro*," I answered, dropping fifty cents into his tip jar. "Supersize me."

I was stuffing my face at a picnic table when the horses came onto the racetrack for the first race. The jockeys—none of them any bigger than me—paraded those huge Thoroughbreds past the grandstand.

Dag even had a colt in the race that I recognized. One I'd walked the day before.

Then the jockeys jogged their horses over to the starting gate on the far side of that one-mile track. Lots of people moved up closer to the outer rail for a better look, and so did I.

"The final horse moves into line," echoed the track announcer's voice. "And they're off!"

Suddenly, voices began buzzing all around me in that crowd.

People were hollering, clapping, and whistling for the horses they'd bet on to cross the finish line first.

"Let's go, number six!" screamed some fatso, slamming his program against his palm, like that would make his horse run faster. "Let's go!"

The field raced around the far turn, maybe a quarter mile away, still too small to really see. Then they turned into the homestretch, running straight toward me and getting bigger with every stride.

Dag's colt was in front, with two other horses breathing down his neck.

I could hear their hooves thundering across the hard ground.

Another horse charged up from the outside, but Dag's colt wouldn't let him by.

The rider on Dag's colt was pumping his arms, and I could feel mine moving too.

The sweat was starting at my temples, and at the first *crack* of the whip I swear my heart skipped a beat.

My toes pressed into the ground, with my weight leaning forward. I felt as excited as the first time I ever galloped a horse with Mom.

Then twenty yards from the finish, as he raced past where I was standing by the rail, Dag's colt took a bad step. He lunged inside, and I lost my balance along with that jockey.

I was pulling back on the imaginary reins, trying to gain control, when a hand grabbed my shoulder from behind.

"Hey, Gas," Tammie said as I nearly fell backward into her arms.

Chapter Six

TAMMIE TOOK ME ON a tour of the racetrack's grandstand and told me how she was in college at the University of Arkansas.

"That's in Fayetteville, close to where I live with my mom," she said. "I'll be starting my second year there soon, studying animal science. But I've spent every summer here with Grandpa since I was twelve. That's what I love best, riding and taking care of the horses."

Her voice trailed off, like it was my turn to tell something about myself.

"I'm from Texas. That's the second-biggest state there is," I told her. "And I've been riding horses for a while now."

Then I saw the flashing lights from the arcade games against the back wall of the grandstand, and instead of telling

Tammie any more, I said, "Come on, I'll challenge you at any game you want."

For fifty cents a ride Tammie and me climbed aboard two big plastic horses and raced each other around a track that was projected onto a video screen.

"Don't try to come up on the inside of me," she said, smiling. "I'll put you over the rail."

"You've been hanging around El Diablo too long," I told her.

By our third game I'd really got the hang of it. We set the screen for Churchill Downs and raced against each other in the Kentucky Derby, with eighteen other horses in our way.

We both broke our horses fast from the starting gate and were running neck and neck going into the first turn.

I took my eyes off the screen for a second, just to look over at her.

Even with her teeth clenched and lower lip curled up as she tried to leave me in her dust, I thought she was the sexiest girl I'd ever seen. And every part of me was screaming out for her.

Tammie got ahead of me coming off the turn, starting down the backstretch. I began pumping my arms quicker, trying to catch up. Then, heading into the far turn, I pulled almost even with her again.

As we raced into the homestretch, there was just one other horse in front of us.

"Let me show you what it takes," she said, breathing harder. "You just have to want it bad enough."

"That's me," I said.

She was rocking furiously in the saddle and so was I. We both zipped past that horse in the lead like it was standing still. I was pumping away on instinct, without a clear thought in my mind.

Then, with a hundred yards to go, Tammie went to the fake whip, slapping at her horse's right side. She brushed my shoulder by accident with its long cellophane straps, and that sent a chill down my spine.

I could see the finish line and *had* to get there first. I pushed with all my might, harder and harder, and in the final stride I let out an *"Aaggghhhh"* as I shoved my horse's long neck forward.

Bells went off on my side of the game. And I watched a bead of sweat drip down Tammie's cheek to the corner of her mouth.

On the video screen a beauty queen came rushing out of the crowd and draped a blanket of red roses across my horse.

"Well?" I asked, still panting.

"Can't believe you won, Gas," she answered. "Last summer

I did this a dozen times with my boyfriend, and he didn't beat me once."

That word "boyfriend" stuck in my chest, like Tammie had just slammed me with a claw hammer.

"But he'd never been on a racehorse in his life. Not like you have," she said. "Anyway, I haven't seen him since he went back to school in September—almost a year now."

That's when I knew I had to find a way to get back on a horse for *real*.

The people who worked at the hothouse with Mom made a five-foot cross out of purple flowers for her funeral. Right down the center of it, in yellow roses, they spelled out her name: M-A-R-I-A.

The morning after she was buried, I got up early and went to the cemetery alone, while Dad slept off the whiskey he'd drunk. There wasn't anything to mark her grave yet, just a rectangle of soft brown dirt where the grass was missing. The wind had scattered most of the flowers we'd left, and even that big cross was down on its side. But I stood it back up where a headstone should be, shoving the cross's metal stand deep into the ground so it couldn't get blown over again.

It was the tallest marker of any grave there, and you could

see it from all the way down the hill and outside the wrought-iron fence.

I'd closed my eyes and smelled those roses.

It was just like having some part of Mom there with me.

I visited her for nine days straight and even started dragging a garden hose over from a workers' station to spray those roses with water. But after the first week they were all wilting. Then the wind stripped lots of petals away, and I could see the Styrofoam skeleton of that cross underneath.

I took one of those roses home, pressing it between the pages of Mom's Bible, right at the start of her favorite story, about Adam and Eve.

Only, Dad was pissed off when he realized where I'd been going.

"You think she loved you more than me? That why you go there by yourself?" asked Dad, smelling of alcohol. "We're family, you and me. You don't do that to family. Cut me out that way."

A few hours later, when he was much drunker, Dad took a swing at me. That was the first time he ever hit me, and it was the first and last time I ever swung back.

I wound up my arm, pulling it back as far as it could go.

Then I closed my eyes and let my fist fly.

"Is that all you got, Gas?" he said. "What? She never taught you how to fight? You went to her for everything *else*."

"Don't say that!" I screamed as his arms swallowed up my punches.

Hitting him didn't make me feel any better. It made me feel even smaller and weaker.

When it was over, I had a mouse under my right eye that turned black and blue by morning. I felt so bad over what Dad had said that I didn't go back to the cemetery for two days.

But the next time I went, that cross was gone.

The groundskeepers must have thought it was garbage, because I found it sitting upside down in one of their green trash bins, snapped in two.

In my heart I blamed Dad for that.

Tammie's grandpa had a filly entered a few races down the line, so she started back toward his barn to help get her ready.

"Rose of Sharon's running in that same race. It looks like she's in way over her head today. But you can never tell with Dag and his bag of tricks," she said, walking away. "Hey, maybe we can have a rematch, me and you, out on the track in the morning sometime, exercising horses."

"It'll just turn out the same," I said, wondering how long I could pretend I knew how to ride. "With me winning."

"You wish," Tammie said.

After that I headed back to Dag's barn, thinking I could help bring Rose of Sharon over to the racetrack and see some more of Tammie when she got there with her grandpa's filly.

But when I came up on the barn, Paolo was in front of the only open door with both arms folded across his chest, like he was standing guard. And Nacho was sitting outside on top of a turned-over bucket, waiting with an empty lead shank in his hands.

"*Gringo,*" said Paolo in a harsh voice. "Why you here? No work for you now."

I glanced over at Nacho, but he looked lost sitting there, like he didn't know why he wasn't inside the barn.

"Just thought I could do something," I said. "Help out."

"Oh, you a big help, little man," Paolo snorted. "The boss very busy inside. Prerace inspection. No one allowed in."

A few minutes later Dag came into the doorway, giving Paolo a big thumbs-up.

"*Está preparada,*" Paolo told Nacho, who went into Rose of Sharon's stall and attached the lead shank to her bridle for the walk over to the front side.

Only, Rose of Sharon wasn't the same easygoing filly anymore. She was suddenly a bundle of energy, and Nacho had to wrestle with her every step of the way to the track. He kept trying to calm her down, stroking Rose of Sharon's head and whispering to her in Spanish.

I couldn't tell if she was just pumped up because she knew she was going to race, or if something else was going on.

There was a walking ring in the paddock, just off the grandstand, where the crowd gathered to see the horses get saddled. Tammie took one look at Rose of Sharon and shook her head.

"See that odds board, Gas?" she said. "Rose of Sharon should be at least ten to one in this race. But she's only three to one. Guess why? 'Cause Dag's probably got a bundle of money down on this one. Just look at her on the walking ring, ready to explode. She's been milk-shaked for sure."

"What does that mean—'milk-shaked'?" I asked.

"A milk shake's a mix of baking soda and Gatorade. The sugar gives a horse a burst of energy, and the sodium fights off muscle fatigue so they keep running. A trainer or somebody sticks a long tube into a horse's nose, right down into the stomach, and pumps it in. Only, nobody really knows how much to give a horse. How much will make it run faster, and how much will make it sick. Because that's what horses do. They don't puke things up like people. They just get sick."

"Then, how come the track doesn't catch him at it, like they did El Diablo fixing races?" I asked.

"Because by the time a horse gets to the test barn after the race, all that stuff's been burned up out of its system. That's why. There's a special test for high levels of carbon dioxide left over from the baking soda. But they don't give that one at Pennington. It costs too much," she said, getting more aggravated with every word. "Honest trainers can't compete with crooks like Dag. That's what happened to most of my grandpa's horses. Their owners moved them over to Dag's barn so their horses could be with a *winner*."

I watched Tammie's grandpa go over every inch of their filly, stretching out her front legs one at a time and making sure everything was right with her before he tacked on the saddle.

Dag never even looked at Rose of Sharon. He spent the whole time in the paddock schmoozing with her owners and giving instructions to the jockey—a hawk-nosed guy named Gillette—while Paolo put the saddle on her.

In the race Rose of Sharon shot right out of the starting gate for the lead. But she had company as another filly pressed her all the way, making her run hard.

"The field moves for the far turn, and a speed duel starts to percolate on the front end," called the track announcer.

The crowd gasped when the time for the first quarter mile was posted.

"Twenty-one and three-fifths seconds! That's way too fast!" screamed some guy with a fistful of betting tickets. "She's cooked!"

But at the head of the homestretch Gillette shook the reins at Rose of Sharon, who spurted clear. Then I saw Cap's filly, flying up fast on the outside.

"There's an eighth of a mile to go, and here comes My Heavenly Sign, a fresh challenger for Rose of Sharon, who's had to run hard the whole way. Now it's My Heavenly Sign right at the throatlatch of Rose of Sharon," called the announcer.

Tammie was jumping up and down, screaming, "Come on, baby! Come on!"

I would have bet my life that Cap's filly was going to run right on by, and probably everybody else in that grandstand would have too. Except maybe for Dag.

"Seventy yards to go, and the resilient Rose of Sharon's got another gear," said the announcer. "She pulls away from My Heavenly Sign. They come under the wire, and it's going to be Rose of Sharon, who would NOT BE DENIED!"

"You can't train a horse to do *that!*" shouted Tammie as she stormed past Dag.

Then Paolo went over to Nacho, slipping an arm around his shoulder.

"La chica es bonita, pero muy loca en la cabeza," Paolo said, twirling a finger at his right temple.

Chapter Seven

Early the next morning Dag was standing out in front of his barn screaming for Nacho.

"Today, kid! Let's go! Where's Bad Boy Rising?" boomed Dag, beside a pair of horses ready to head down to the racetrack.

El Diablo was perched on one of them, smirking.

"Ahora, estúpido!" Paolo barked toward the barn.

That's when Nacho brought out Bad Boy Rising, without a saddle or an exercise rider.

"What the hell? Where's that new rider I hired? I'll fire his worthless ass," Dag hissed.

"Don't know," said Paolo. "Saw him in the cantina last night with a bottle of tequila and *una blanca fea.*"

"We'll have to work out Bad Boy with the next set of horses," Dag said, shaking his head.

"Not me," warned El Diablo. "I don't get on wack jobs. He's got no talent and too many screws loose."

I knew this was my chance to jump over all those beaners at the barn, and impress Tammie, too. I was scared to death of Bad Boy Rising, but I couldn't let it slip by.

"I'll ride," I said, pulling up every ounce of courage I had.

Paolo burst out laughing over that, but El Diablo grilled the shit out of me with a stare, like I'd just shown him up.

Dag hesitated for a few seconds before he said, "Ya know what? You got two minutes to get a saddle, a protective vest, and a helmet from the equipment room. Then if you can get on that beast, you can ride him."

After I got ready, Nacho gave me a leg up onto Bad Boy's back.

"*Vaya con Dios,*" he whispered.

I knew that meant "Go with God" from the times I'd heard Mom singing an old song with those same words:

Vaya con Dios, my darling,
Vaya con Dios, my love.

I probably only got Bad Boy Rising to the racetrack because that's where he wanted to go anyway.

Then I guided him through the open gap in the rail, which was lined by an ambulance on each side—one with a trailer attached to the back for the horses, and a human one for jockeys.

"The three of you, jog your horses over to the half-mile pole, and then let 'em break running to the wire together," Dag called out to us.

Just then Tammie came galloping past, her ponytail flying in the breeze and the whip sticking out of the back pocket of her blue jeans.

As I caught her eye, Tammie smiled and smooched to her horse, "Mcch, mcch."

"Think you can be a rider 'cause you short and skinny?" cracked El Diablo on our way over to that pole. "Takes more than that, *pequeño*. Lot more."

My heart was already beating a mile a minute by the time I turned Bad Boy Rising loose. He started sprinting at full speed, sandwiched between those other two horses. His head was shooting straight back like a piston, right at mine.

I was just trying to keep my balance, praying to hold on.

El Diablo was riding to my outside.

Coming off the turn, he leaned in and hollered, "Yahhh!"

Bad Boy spooked and nearly ran out from underneath me.

But I had a death grip on a handful of his mane, and I

71

stayed in the saddle. When we flashed past the wire, I pulled back on the reins as hard as I could. But Bad Boy Rising only stopped running when *he* was ready to quit.

After I'd caught my breath and my lungs stopped hurting, I saw that my knuckles had turned pure white from squeezing the reins so tight.

"You got some raw talent," Dag told me. "Maybe I could use you for some things."

Part of me was satisfied because I'd done it. I'd hung on to that demon, a horse even El Diablo didn't want to ride. But another part of me could hear in Dag's voice what I'd heard in Mrs. Mallory's, our high school drama teacher, when she recruited me *special* for the school play.

"I've had my eye on you for a while now, Gas. I think you could be a valuable part of this production," she said.

I went home on cloud nine, thinking how actors like Tom Cruise were shorter than everybody else around them in their movies.

Then the next day I found out that she needed me to play a Munchkin in *The Wizard of Oz,* and even thought I could handle two roles and be one of the Wicked Witch's little monkeys with wings, too. But I never showed up for rehearsal or answered the notes she left for me in homeroom.

Later that morning, after I'd finished walking my last horse, Dag sent me over to the racing office. A man there fingerprinted me and used the information on my yellow ID card to issue me a temporary jockey's license.

I couldn't believe it. I held that paper by the corners so any ink left on my fingers wouldn't smudge a single line.

That was the first thing I ever got in my whole life for being small. And I didn't even want to fold it up to fit inside my wallet.

I showed the artist who ran the tattoo parlor my fake ID, and the first thing he said was, "Kid, it's not my job to talk people *out* of getting tattoos. But at your age it's a risk to put a girl's name on your arm. Two weeks later she's left you for somebody new, and you get to see how big an idiot you were every day in the mirror."

"She's already gone," I told him. "It's for my mom."

That's when he pulled up his shirt and showed me *his* mother's name surrounded by two angels blowing trumpets over his heart.

The artist sketched out the cross on a pad for me with the letters of Mom's name running down the middle. That part was simple. But he worked for almost forty-five minutes drawing in the petals from all the flowers and roses until he got it just right.

The picture got transferred onto my right bicep with a stencil. Only, it looked cold on my arm without any color to it.

He poured caps of black, purple, and yellow ink, and took some sharp needles out of a bag.

"Concentrate on breathing slow," he told me, putting on a pair of rubber gloves. "Every now and then somebody passes out. It's not from the pain. It's because they forget to breathe."

The machine that held the needle started buzzing louder than the neon sign in the front window, and I could feel the needle digging into my skin. But it wasn't even close to the pain I'd been feeling. And when that tattoo was finished, I knew I'd have it in my life forever, no matter what.

I sat in something that looked like a dentist's chair, gritting my teeth and looking up at the drawings that lined the walls.

There were cute teddy bears, skulls, bloody daggers with snakes curled around the handles, a marijuana leaf, a bald eagle gripping lightning bolts in its claws, and even a snoring beaner taking a siesta under a big sombrero.

Dad had a tiny tattoo on the inside of his forearm, from his days in the navy. It was of a hula-dancing girl wearing a grass skirt. And whenever he flexed his muscles, she'd shake her hips.

I wouldn't look down at my arm anymore, not until that artist was done. But some woman came in off the street with butterflies tattooed on her wrists and ankles. She sat there watching him do the colors for a few minutes before she said, "That's just gorgeous. I can almost smell those yellow roses."

When that buzzing stopped and the artist flipped up his safety glasses, I finally looked.

That tattoo was so beautiful it nearly broke my heart when he had to cover it with a big bandage. But he warned me, "It's an open wound, and you've got to take real precautions for a while."

So I took care of it like he explained. I kept it moist with baby lotion, and I didn't pick at any of the little scabs, no matter how much they itched.

I went to find Tammie at her grandpa's barn so I could show her my jockey's license. Cap was standing at the door, looking inside at his row of four horses beside a dozen empty stalls.

"Tammie's not here right now," he said, barely shifting his eyes.

The feeling inside Cap's barn was different than Dag's.

There was a calmness here, and standing next to Cap, I could feel it seeping into my bones.

"I guess you grew up around racehorses," I said.

"No, not me. I was raised in Chicago by my father, a photographer. My mother died before I was old enough to remember her," Cap said. "But I'd see horses every day on the streets pulling ice wagons. Before electric refrigerators, people needed ice for their iceboxes, to keep the food cold. Anyway, I'd pet those horses, feeding them sugar and such. Then one day a driver left the hand brake off in his wagon, and a horse followed me all the way to school. I thought that horse loved *me*. I never considered it was the sugar in my pocket."

That's when I showed him my license.

"Dag arrange that for you?" he asked like he already knew the answer.

I just nodded my head.

"I saw you ride this morning, and the best thing I can say about it is that you're still in one piece. I think you know that too. So I'm not sure what that snake sees in you. Don't think I'm just against him because the horses that used to fill these stalls are in *his* barn now," said Cap. "But Gas, let me ask you. Where's your family?"

I'm not exactly sure why I started to tell him the truth.

There was something behind his eyes that kept them steady while he talked. Something that said he wasn't going anywhere. That he wasn't going to move off the spot he was standing on, not unless he was good and ready.

The only person I ever knew like that before was Mom.

"My mother was killed back in March, around Easter time," I said. "After that it's just my dad. But I don't talk about him much."

"I'm sorry to hear it," Cap said. "Just to say—if Dag hasn't asked you about your family yet, it's probably because he doesn't have to. He can read it all over you."

Then Tammie got there.

"Gas, is that a jockey's license? Congratulations," she said, kissing me on the cheek.

For the second her soft lips were on me, I could feel the blood pulsing through my entire body, and then my face turning flush.

"Grandpa, did you see Gas on the racetrack riding that nut job of a horse with El Diablo leaning all over him?" asked Tammie. "That was gutsy."

"Is that what they call 'crazy' these days?" said Cap, grinning. "Gutsy?"

"Now all you need's a trainer to put you on some live runners in real races," said Tammie.

"Oh, yeah, that's what he needs," said Cap without a trace of a smile. "Some *trainer* doing him a favor."

To celebrate, Tammie took me to the cantina to play Ping-Pong.

I was standing on the other side of the table from her, looking over the net. I wasn't even sure if she liked me as a friend or maybe something more. But a feeling inside me didn't think it was right that I'd told her grandpa about Mom when I hadn't told Tammie yet.

"I'm not at home anymore because my mom died in a car accident," I said fast, like it might hurt less. "All because some illegal Mexican didn't want to get deported."

Then I looked at the beaners everywhere inside that cantina, and I cut the air hard with the paddle in my hand.

"That must be really tough on you, Gas," she said soft, following where my eyes had just been.

I tap-danced around a few of her questions about Dad before we began to play.

After the first game Tammie picked the ball up off the floor and said, "My parents got divorced when I was six. They don't even talk to each other now. It's sad because it's like they're dead to each other."

Chapter Eight

I WAS WALKING ROSE of Sharon in the courtyard beneath the branches of that big shade tree the next morning when Nacho and Anibal came running over.

"Here. See," Nacho said, pushing a long sheet of paper at me. "*Mañana*. You ride Bad Boy. Tomorrow, race number three."

It was the entries for the next day's races, and there was my name listed as the jockey for Bad Boy Rising, with three asterisks next to it.

3RD RACE

PURSE: $2,400

6 FURLONGS, (CLAIMING $2,000)

FOR 3-YEAR-OLDS & UP

Horse	Jockey	Weight
1. Sly Old Fox	Gillette	118
2. Road Not Traveled	Castro	118
3. Langhorne Express	Samuel	118
4. Bad Boy Rising	Giambanco Jr.***	108
5. Key to the Garden	Ramos	118
6. Deep Water	Clemens	118

I felt six feet tall as I finished walking the last of those laps with Rose of Sharon.

"You should be down-on-your-knees grateful. This is a helluva opportunity," Dag told me later at the barn. "The winner gets sixty percent of the purse money, and the jockey ten percent of that. You could make a hundred and a half for about a minute and fourteen seconds' worth of work. And that's the cheapest purse money we run for around here. Now see yourself riding all nine races, every day. Start to add up that scratch."

"I appreciate it. I'll do the best I can," I said, with Cap's warning about Dag creeping into my brain.

"I know you will, Gas," said Dag, taking the toothpick out of his mouth and stabbing at the air between us.

"What are these three asterisks next to my name for?" I asked.

"Well, one asterisk would mean you're a bug boy. Three says you're a triple bug boy—the lowest of the low in a jockey's career. You got no real experience, and to even make it a race, the other jocks have to spot you ten pounds of weight. But if either you or the horse you're riding has got any talent, it can be a big advantage."

That's when El Diablo came over and stood at my shoulder.

"Satan himself is gonna give you some pointers on how to ride for me," said Dag.

"Four o'clock, I meet you right here, bug," said El Diablo in a disgusted voice, like Dag had forced him into it.

I walked away still feeling great, except for the parts about me being tutored by El Diablo, and being called a *bug*. And somewhere in my mind I had a vision of myself squished under the sole of somebody's shoe.

"Oh, and Gas," Dag called after me. "No matter what you might hear about me from certain people at this racetrack, don't forget, I'm the only one who's taking care of you."

That afternoon I went over to the racetrack. I watched the

jockeys parade their horses before every race, dressed in the different colored silks of each horse's owner.

People in the grandstand would yell all kinds of things to them:

"Go get 'em, Jorge! Bring this one home! You're my boy!"

"Use that whip, Chop-Chop!"

"I lost a fortune betting on you, Gillette. And every time I bet somebody else, you beat me, you bastard!"

"You on the number six horse, you're a bum with a capital *B*!"

Sometimes those riders would wink at the good comments or spit on the ground over the real bad ones. But they mostly stared straight ahead, pretending those people weren't even there.

It was like they were little supermen, and nothing anybody said could touch them. That's how I wanted to be.

Nobody in that crowd had the guts to climb aboard a 1,200-pound Thoroughbred like those jockeys did, driving them through tiny openings between horses that could close up in a split second. And even if somebody there did, they were probably too big and heavy to race-ride.

It was just after three thirty when I watched the horses in the fifth race go flying past. With the sound of their hoofbeats thundering in my ears and a streak of bravery running through me, I walked up to the first pay phone I saw to call Dad.

It had been five days since I left, and I had to know what he'd say. Even if he put me down, like I knew he might, I had that jockey's license I could hold over his head, without telling him where I was.

I listened to the operator's voice and to a dollar forty in change slide through the coin slot. Then, with my heart pounding, I got connected and heard the phone ring in my house.

Ring . . . ring . . . ring . . .

After three rings Mom's voice used to pick up on the answering machine. For months after she got killed, it still did.

"You've reached the home of the Giambancos—Gaston, Maria, and Gaston Jr. Leave a message at the tone. We'll get back to you soon, and have a terrific day," she'd say.

Our last name always sounded like music out of Mom's mouth—"Gi-am-ban-co."

Last semester, when I didn't know how I'd get through the day, I'd call home from school just to hear that message. I'd close my eyes, listening to the sound of her voice. In my mind I could always see her galloping a horse at sunset, with the sky a mix of bright blue and orange.

Then late one night the phone started ringing, and neither Dad or me got to it in time. Her voice came on. Dad was so angry to hear it that he slammed the answering machine with his fist, breaking it in two.

And the last trace of her was gone for good.

I let the phone ring at least twenty times that afternoon from the racetrack, but Dad never answered and no message came on.

Before I hung up, I dropped my face into my chest to hold back the tears and stop the feeling that there was no place left for me anywhere.

When I got to Dag's barn, El Diablo was already there, sitting on a bale of hay with a whip in one hand and an open can of beer in the other.

Nacho, Rafael, and Anibal were there too, for the horses' four o'clock feeding.

"*This* your horse now, bug," said El Diablo, standing up and slapping at that bale of hay with his whip. "Climb on."

I felt stupid, but I did it anyway.

Nacho and his brothers were already grinning at me.

"First, starting gate. You break a horse from there? Ever?" El Diablo asked.

I shook my head.

"It called iron monster, 'cause you don't know what a horse

do inside there. They can get scared in that tight space—the size of a phone booth. They turn loco on you," El Diablo said. "Keep your horse leaning against back doors, no the front. So he no flip backward and come down on top of you. Crush you. Snap your spine."

I leaned all my weight back.

"RINNNNNGGGGG!" he shouted in my ear, like the sound of the bell on the starting gate when the iron doors spring open.

My heart jumped, and my weight shot forward.

"Now you go from the gate. Push with your arms. Pump hard. Use your legs for balance," he demanded, with his face two inches from mine, and the smell of beer heavy on his breath.

I was pumping away when Rafael came over with a handful of feed and offered it to my hay bale.

"No fucking joke!" snapped El Diablo, raising his whip toward Rafael for a second.

He turned back to me and said, "Bug, you learn to ride right or you kill somebody out there. Somebody with kids, you know. I ride a million times better than you, and I kill my own brother on the track in my country—Peru."

Then El Diablo poured some beer into the dirt, watching it seep into the earth.

"That's for *him*—*mi hermano*," El Diablo said. *"Por el muerto*. For the dead."

"How'd it happen?" I asked, cautious.

"How?" he answered, stopping to take a slug of beer. "His horse break a leg on the first turn. So my brother jump off. He lying on the ground, but my horse no see. Steps on him. Puts its hoof through his skull. *That's how!"*

I just stared into his glowing eyes.

"I know right away he dead. But I finish the race, not to face it for another minute. I beat my horse with the whip till somebody take it away from me. That's when they give me this name—the Devil."

"But it was an accident," I said.

"That's what I say to my ma-ma when I tell her how I kill her son. That no stop her tears," he said. "Being a jockey 'bout waiting your turn to get hurt, or paralyze, or killed. You know 'bout those things, bug?"

"I know," I answered.

"What you know?" he exploded. "Pick up you shirt! Pick it up! Show me!"

I started to lift my shirt, and El Diablo yanked it quick up to my chin, feeling around my shoulder blades on both sides.

"Hah! Too clean!" he sneered, pulling up his own shirt

and pointing to the bumps beneath his shoulders. "I break each collarbone twice. That's what happens when you go flying from horse. It's a badge of honor for riders. I got four. It say I know 'bout being jockey, 'bout what can happen. You got none, bug. You know nothing. You no even got a pair of leather boots. You ride in joke sneakers your ma-ma buy for you."

I was somewhere between being ready to break down bawling and wanting to fight. Then I thought about those jockeys on the racetrack and how they seemed bulletproof to all that shit people said to them.

That's when Nacho yelled at El Diablo in Spanish.

I heard him say my name, the word *"madre,"* and *"no."*

But El Diablo just laughed him off.

"What else you got to teach me?" I asked, trying to sound strong.

"You know how to use this?" he came back, shoving the whip at me.

I closed my hand around it, and the inside of my palm started to burn.

"Prove to me," said El Diablo.

I hit that hay bale as hard as I could, still pumping with my other arm.

I could hear the *swoosh* of air and almost feel the whip's crack.

"Now, switch whip to your left hand," he ordered. "That surprises horse. Lets him know you mean business."

But I didn't have nearly as much strength from that side.

"Harder! Hit harder!" he hollered, grabbing my left arm and squeezing until it hurt.

Then he swung my arm up and down, again and again, until I thought he was going to break it off.

But I wouldn't give in or tell him to stop. I just stared right through him.

Nacho and his brothers came rushing over, pulling El Diablo off me, screaming, *"Para! Para! No!"*

El Diablo just shoved the three of them to the floor, with the horses in the barn raising their voices too.

I jumped off that bale of hay and stuck my chest out in front of his, with every muscle in my body trembling.

"Back off!" I shouted in the strongest voice I could find.

Then he looked into my eyes, nearly breathing fire, and said, "They take my license for making one mistake. Now I got to beg every year to ride—to be somebody again. And they let *you* ride, bug. *You?*"

"But *I* didn't do anything wrong," I said, and it was

like a thousand-pound weight was suddenly lifted off my shoulders.

"Forget what I teach you 'bout riding. You want to be jockey? No make the mistake I make. 'Cause then you be crushed anyway," he said. "Lesson over."

As he left, El Diablo kicked the beer can lying on the ground. And with a stinging welt rising up on my left arm, I went over to where that can had landed and kicked it even harder.

After they got up and dusted themselves off, I walked back to the dorms with Nacho, Rafael, and Anibal.

They were mad as hornets, cursing at El Diablo in Spanish.

"*Ve?* See this?" Rafael asked me, annoyed, pointing to the bloody scrape on his chin. "This for helping you."

"Next time, Gas, fight devil you-self," said Anibal. "So we no get fired."

Nacho was walking with his head down and hadn't said a word to me.

Part of me couldn't stand what those beaners had done. Like I needed *them* for protection. But there they were, the only ones by my side.

So I wasn't sure how to act or what to say. And I didn't

know if I could trust any kind of good feelings I had for what they'd done.

"*Gracias,*" I told them before I pushed it all out of my mind.

Chapter Nine

I WAS RESTLESS IN bed that whole night, stressing over El Diablo and riding in my first real race. I was sweating under the covers and slipped out of my sleep at least a dozen times, halfway between dreaming and being awake. I couldn't remember a single one of those dreams, only the sound of the things hammering at me.

An alarm from the hall went off at four forty-five, and the rain was beating down on Pennington Racetrack in buckets.

"You be water bug today, *gringo*," sneered Paolo at the barn.

The track had turned into a muddy sea of slop, and Dag sent just a couple of horses out to train on it. That meant the rest of the horses got walked inside the barn to stretch their legs. And they were probably happy to get at least that much exercise.

It doesn't matter that Thoroughbreds are born to run, most of them spend nearly twenty-three hours a day cramped up in their stalls, aching for a chance to get turned loose.

That's why I knew Mom would have felt sorry for every horse stabled at Pennington.

Bad Boy Rising had been his usual nasty self, charging his stall door and kicking at the walls most of the morning.

I saw El Diablo leaving Dag's office, and for a second my heart stood still. But I planted both feet beneath me, and I wouldn't sidestep him.

El Diablo stopped in his tracks, looking almost embarrassed over what had happened. Then he took a long breath and focused his eyes just below mine.

That was exactly how Dad looked after the first time he'd smacked me and had a chance to sober up.

El Diablo's lips pushed together, and I thought maybe he was about to apologize. Then, suddenly, I saw the anger building in his face as his dark cheeks stiffened.

Only, I couldn't figure out if he was mad at himself or me.

"Bug, no kill yourself or anybody else out there," he said before he turned around and headed out of the barn.

"I won't," I said.

By the time those words had left my mouth, El Diablo

was out the door, walking through the pouring rain to his car.

Underneath my shirt, on my left arm, I could feel the purple bruise from him, which was nearly as big as my tattoo.

Then I heard his engine start up, and El Diablo pulled away.

The rain never let up that morning. So no one walked their horses in the courtyard, and that meant no Tammie.

At around eleven o'clock, with most of the horses put away, Dag called me into his office.

"Those are for you," he said, pointing to a pair of black leather boots trimmed with red and yellow flames on his desk. "El Diablo left them."

"He did?" I said, surprised.

"You didn't think you were going to ride in sneakers, did you?" he asked.

"No," I answered.

"Take the rest of the equipment you need from here— helmet, saddle, a protective vest. Then go over to the jockeys' room and learn their routine. The clerk of scales, he runs the place. He'll assign you a valet."

"A what?" I asked.

"A valet. He'll shine your boots, carry your saddle, wipe your nose *and* your ass if you need him to. That's his job. He's your mama and papa in that room, all rolled into one," Dag said.

I'd noticed there was no webbing in front of Bad Boy's stall, and asked Dag why he was eating before a race.

"It won't matter. He's just racing for the exercise today. I'm trying to get him into shape—the same as you. So let him eat up. He couldn't get any slower," said Dag, poking a finger into my shoulder. "But I see you learn fast. Just remember, *I* do the training here, not *you*. You only got a shot at this 'cause I went out on a real limb for you, fudging your age. That's what lets you live and work here, *being eighteen*. That's what got you being a jockey, too. Or else you'd be dealin' with whatever you ran away from back home."

"Okay," I said, picking El Diablo's boots up off of Dag's desk.

Before I left, I stood in front of Bad Boy's stall watching him dig into his feed bucket. He wasn't the least bit interested in making friends. And if that monster weren't so hungry, he'd have probably been trying to bite me with those huge white teeth.

Then I saw the flutter of wings behind Bad Boy, and I had to look twice. A family of sparrows had nested in a deep crack running down the back wall of his stall.

I guess he didn't mind them being there, because he'd never chased them out. And having sparrows for company was probably better than spending time with Dag's chicken that walked backward.

I showed my license and signed in at the jockeys' room. Then the clerk of scales assigned me an old, gray black man named Parker as a valet.

He was bent over at the waist, and that put him at my height.

Parker shook my hand and called me "boss."

"I handle another rider too—Gillette. That's where my money is," he said. "I call him 'chief.' But I only got one Lord. That's the big man upstairs. So I tell the truth. If your riding's for shit, I won't lie to you."

"Why don't you just call me Gas," I told him.

"Because you're the boss and I'm the *hoss*," Parker said, picking up the bag with my equipment in it.

We passed through the swinging doors and into a big locker room. There were seven or eight jockeys there already, all grown men, eyeballing me as I followed behind Parker to a tall, empty locker.

"Steam room's to the left if you need it. Bathroom's on the

right. There's a pool table over there to kill time. And if you get hungry, there's a food counter from where we just came, out by the main scale," said Parker, pointing his finger like a compass needle.

"That's all right, I brought my lunch," I said, unwrapping a submarine sandwich and putting a can of soda on the stool in front of me.

"No, boss. You don't take a bite before you weigh in," Parker warned me. "I'd be careful about bringing *that* kind of food in here."

I started to ask why, but there were already three or four riders marching over to make sure I knew all the answers.

"Whatcha eatin', bug?" asked one of them.

Before I could open my mouth, Gillette said, "You know, most of us survive on one lousy meal a day, and we still gotta sit in that steam room sweatin' our asses off to lose weight."

"It's his first time, chief," said Parker. "He don't know no better."

"Yeah? First ride, bug?" asked a jock named Castro. "You gonna get one of us hurt in that third race? Maybe we *sandwich* you coming out of the starting gate so we don't have to worry."

That's when Parker pulled those riding boots out of my bag, and everybody saw the flames painted on them.

"You usually got to kill a rider to get his boots," said Castro. "Or do him a mighty big favor."

"You know, I'm the one who testified against El Diablo at the hearing. How he asked me to hold my horse back too," said Gillette, with his eyes piercing through me. "Did he send you here to give me a little shove over the rail to get even?"

"It's not like that," I said. "He lent them to me 'cause I didn't have a pair of my own."

"He *lent* them to you," laughed one of the riders. "El Diablo?"

"It's true. I walk horses in the mornings for Dag. That's where my saddle and everything else came from. I just want to be a jockey. That's all."

"We'll see if you got what it takes, bug," said Castro.

"You watch him close, Parker," demanded Gillette, as him and the other jockeys walked off.

"Yes, chief," answered Parker.

Then a voice came over the loudspeaker: "Giambanco Jr., report up front to get weighed."

"Strip down to your shorts, boss," Parker told me.

But when I took my shirt off, Parker said, "Jesus! What's that on your arm?"

"That's a tattoo for my mom's memory," I answered.

"I know what a *tattoo* is," he said. "I meant your other arm."

I was ready to lie like I always did. But I believed Parker when he said that he'd only tell me the truth. Maybe I'd been searching for somebody to say something like that for five long months.

"El Diablo was drunk yesterday and he nearly broke my arm off," I said without holding back.

That was the first time I ever admitted to anybody I'd been hit.

The first time Dad saw my tattoo, I was coming out of the shower.

"Gas, you got a towel on?" he hollered, banging at the bathroom door.

I'd been hiding it from him for more than a week, but the word "Yeah" slipped out of my mouth before I could pull it back.

He stood there staring at it, with his hand glued to the doorknob.

Then he glared at me like I was a stranger who'd sneaked into his house and stolen something.

"When I got this," he exploded, pointing to the hula girl

on his forearm, "I hadn't even met your mother yet! I was a stupid kid!"

He hit the bathroom door one time, and I felt my knees buckle.

"But she never minded," he kept on. "I even told her I'd put her name under it. But she said no."

Dad was stone sober. Only, it didn't matter.

I could see the rage and pain building up inside him, until he was almost on some other planet. So I didn't try to reason with him.

"You're not old enough to do that without my permission," he seethed. "It's a crime. I'll sue the bastard who gave it to you."

"You can't," I said, with the water still dripping down my legs onto the floor. "I fooled him with a fake ID."

"No! He knew!" he screamed. "Their lowlife kind—*they* all know!"

That's when Dad put his fist through the bathroom door with a *crack*.

He pulled his arm back and sucked the blood right off the tops of his cut knuckles. Then Dad left, cursing himself.

I didn't know why he was so jealous over Mom, or why everything that meant so much to me pushed him further away.

But I looked at the splintered door like he'd punched a hole in my heart. And I started to realize that Dad didn't have to lay a finger on me anymore to hurt me.

Once I checked into the jockeys' room, I wasn't allowed to leave, except to ride in my race.

"No phone calls, unless I'm there to monitor them. And I have to approve all visitors," the clerk of scales told me as I stepped onto the scale and he recorded my weight at 105 pounds.

"Why the prison treatment?" I asked.

"Anybody can grab you walking around this racetrack and threaten you into holding your horse back, boss," Parker answered for him.

"You don't take money from people either," the clerk said as he went over my name, birthday, and address with me. "Since you're eighteen, you can bet, but only on the horse *you're* riding. Nobody else's."

"If I wasn't eighteen, I wouldn't be riding, right?" I asked.

"No, you can ride at sixteen in Arkansas, work on the racetrack, too," the clerk answered. "You can't live in those backstretch dorms like you do unless you're eighteen."

I felt the sharp twinge of how Dag had lied to me.

"Who do I notify in case of injury?" the clerk asked. "Any family?"

That question bounced around my brain for a few seconds, and it stung like hell to finally say, "Dag. I mean, trainer Damon Dagget."

I watched the first two races on a TV monitor in the jockeys' room. Gillette won them both, with Parker carrying his saddle back and forth.

The rain was still pounding down, and the riders all came back with their faces and silks splashed with mud.

Twenty-five minutes before the third race Parker put out the owner's silks for me to wear. They were black, with a coiled-up cobra showing its fangs and a forked tongue.

I zipped up the protective vest with all the padding around my ribs and chest, and I felt like a turtle in a shell, carrying its home around on its back.

Then I pulled on those silks and El Diablo's boots.

I looked into the mirror, holding a whip. I hardly recognized myself.

"Here, boss. You'll need three or four pairs of these," said Parker, handing me plastic goggles. "When you get blinded by mud, pull down the top pair and you'll be able to see clear again. That's important to remember."

Right before we went out to ride, the clerk of scales paged my name and said I had a visitor. I walked through the swinging doors, and it was Tammie.

"Is that really you, Gas? All dressed up and ready to race," she said, grabbing both my hands and spreading my arms wide to look at me.

I felt like we were dancing on air together.

The other riders were right on my heels, and Gillette asked, "Tammie, you know this little bug?"

"Gas is a friend of mine. Treat him right," answered Tammie, hugging most of the jocks, who'd ridden for her grandpa.

"You're lucky Tammie says you're okay, bug," said Castro.

"It's one less strike against you," said Gillette. "Now let's see you ride."

Tammie walked me all the way to the paddock gate, and I could feel the pulse of her next to me.

"Go get 'em," she whispered as I stepped inside the paddock alone. "Grandpa and me are rooting for *you*."

Bad Boy Rising was already saddled, with Nacho at his head trying to keep him calm. Paolo was holding a huge umbrella over Dag, like the rain might have melted him.

The other jockeys were busy shaking hands with their horses' owners. Then Dag stuck his hand out to me and said, "I own Bad Boy, Gas. You're wearing my colors."

That's when I took a long look at that cobra on my chest in Dag's mirrored glasses.

"Just push this horse as hard as you can out of the gate. I don't care if he uses everything up early and finishes dead last," Dag said. "Like I told you before, I'm working the two of you into shape."

"Riders up!" called a racing official.

Dag gave me a leg up into the saddle. I tucked the whip under my left arm, and Nacho led Bad Boy Rising and me onto the racetrack.

"Por María," Nacho said as he let us go.

I took a deep breath, nodding my head to him.

The horses paraded past the grandstand. But there weren't any bettors outside in the rain shouting at us. So no one saw that look of steel fixed on my face.

Bad Boy was 25–1 on the odds board. He was a real handful, but I managed to jog him over to the starting gate. An assistant starter grabbed him by the bridle, leading him into stall number three. I leaned Bad Boy up against the back doors like El Diablo told me, so he couldn't flip over. Then I peered through the bars of the doors in front of me, looking as far down the racetrack as I could see.

"One horse left to load," shouted another assistant starter.

I heard the ambulance that was ready to follow behind us rev its engine. Even with all that rain my mouth had gone bone dry.

Suddenly, those iron doors popped opened, and the sound of the bell on the starting gate shot through me like a current.

Bad Boy stumbled on his first step out of the gate, nearly going down to his knees. Time seemed to slip into slow motion all around me as I went tumbling over his head, landing flat on my back in a foot of slop.

The rest of the runners and Bad Boy Rising, who'd righted himself, went splashing down the racetrack.

I felt for my arms and legs, and I was still in one piece. So I pulled my mud-stained goggles down, staring straight up at a gray, sunless sky.

Then I picked myself up off the ground and began the long walk back to the jockeys' room, covered from head to toe in filth, like the bug they said I was.

Chapter Ten

THAT NIGHT I LAY in bed with the lights on. My body was sore as could be, and every part of me, inside and out, ached.

Then, out of nowhere, Nacho started jawing at me.

"No good today, Gas," Nacho said. "You ride ve-ry bad. *Muy malo.*"

"So? What's it to you?" I said with some attitude.

"I Bad Boy's groom," he answered. "No look good. Maybe Señor Dag give me trouble for it."

"Too bad," I told him, with my eyes following along a crack in the ceiling. "Not my problem."

"*Sí*, no *you* problem," Nacho said. "Only *mi, y mis hermanos.*"

"Maybe you need to jump the border to a different country," I said. "One without *me* in it."

"No jump. Crawl. Through a big pipe en de sewer," he said, moving both his hands and feet. "Then run, en de dark. Climb fence. Run more. Always running, running. *Policía* hate us—*muy peligroso.*"

"I'm glad you didn't steal a car," I said, closing my eyes on him.

Anyway, none of Nacho's crap was even close to the heat I'd felt when I got back to that jockeys' room after the race.

"Hey, know what your horse said when he was runnin' around the track without you? 'This feels great! I just got a hundred-pound pimple taken off my ass!'"

Parker was the only one who didn't smile over those wisecracks as he wiped down my saddle.

Tammie kept her distance from me because of the mud.

"It's just one bad ride. Nothing more," she said, standing outside of my reach. "You fall off a horse, you gotta get right back on, *Gi-am-banco*. No fear."

I could almost hear Mom's voice inside of hers.

Right then I wished I had the courage to kiss her on the lips, covered in mud and all. But I didn't.

I was shocked when Dag wasn't steamed at me. He even named me to ride on Rose of Sharon the very next day. Only, she wasn't going to be another 25–1 long shot like Bad Boy

Rising. Dag was dropping her way down in class off that big win three days ago, from $20,000 company into a $10,000 claiming race.

A claiming race is where any trainer or owner can buy one of the horses entered just by writing a check.

Rose of Sharon was listed in the entries as the 2–1 favorite, even with *me* in the saddle. She was supposed to win easy against those cheaper fillies, and probably get claimed for such a bargain price.

"*Señor Dag es loco,*" said Nacho in a stressed voice. "Somebody claim her away—sure. Then I left one horse. One bad horse—Bad Boy."

That's when I pointed to the Scotch-tape outline of that torn-down picture on the wall next to my bed.

"Better than what I got," I said. "You got brothers—family. Me—*nada.* Nothing."

"No *familia* any-where?" he asked. "*Muerto?* All dead?"

I didn't answer and went back to studying that crack in the ceiling.

"You have picture here," Nacho said, tapping his arm where my tattoo would have been. "In you head, no picture? Of you family?"

"Sometimes," I answered.

"Tonight you have this one," he said, handing me the tiny photo of his mother, María.

I only reached out to take it because I saw how serious he was. And when I touched it, it felt like an angel's wings between my fingers.

I wasn't sure where to keep it safe.

Then I took out the Spanish Bible from the top drawer of the nightstand, flipping to the story of Adam and Eve in Genesis, where I'd pressed that dried rose from Mom's cross in our Bible at home.

I recognized it by a little drawing of a man and a woman covered up with fig leaves beneath a tree.

"*La serpiente, que era el más astuto de todos los animales del campo que Jehovah Dios . . .*"

I put the picture between those pages and closed the book shut.

"*Bueno.* She sleep good there," Nacho said before he turned out the light. "Now, you sleep good too, and no fall off my filly tomorrow."

Early the next morning, with the sun breaking through the clouds, Dag had me jog a few horses out on the racetrack. But he wouldn't let me go any faster than that.

"You just concentrate on staying in the saddle. That's all," he told me. "I don't want to risk you getting hurt out there."

I almost couldn't believe his concern.

"I need you to ride that filly today, and I'm entering Bad Boy for tomorrow. He's yours too," said Dag.

"Why me?" I asked. "Didn't Gillette just win on Rose of Sharon?"

"I already told you, I do the training here," hissed Dag. "You just keep your mouth closed and ride, or maybe I'll find some other bug to bless."

Dag didn't wait for any kind of answer. He just walked away from me like he pulled all the strings and I was his little puppet. So I turned my head from side to side, looking all around me with both of my eyes wide open, just to prove to myself it wasn't true.

Later, El Diablo jogged another of Dag's horses alongside the one I was on.

"Thanks for letting me borrow those boots," I said, feeling out his mood. "Sorry I disgraced them like that."

"Pray that's your biggest mistake—falling off horse. That's nothing," El Diablo said. "At least you see ground coming. I fall so far I let you know when I hit bottom."

Then El Diablo broke his horse into a full gallop, leaving me behind.

With the sun beating down on my face, all I could hear in my head was Tammie screaming at Dag after Rose of Sharon's last race, "You can't train a horse to do *that*!"

I didn't know if Dag had pumped her full of one of those magic milk shakes that day she'd won or not. I just knew that I'd be riding her now, and it was going to be my ass on the line.

After the horses got put away that morning, I saw that there was no webbing up in front of Rose of Sharon's stall. That she was filling her stomach just a few hours before she was going to run.

I remembered how it wasn't that way the last time she'd raced.

But I'd learned my lesson and wasn't about to say anything to Dag over it. And I saw Nacho grimace as Paolo tossed another scoop of feed into her bucket.

"Gas, I got a big surprise coming," Tammie said when I saw her walking through the courtyard later. "I just can't say what it is yet."

"Is that some kind of tease?" I asked.

"If that's what you want it to be," she said, winking. "It's really my grandpa's business, so I can't tell. But I'll let you know right after your ride. I promise."

That wink of hers carried me through the early part of the afternoon.

There was a small patch of flowers out in front of the dorms. Most of them were bent over pretty bad from all that rain the day before. Back in Texas we didn't have any dirt surrounding our apartment, just a concrete sidewalk. But Mom always brought seedlings home from her job in the hothouse and planted them in our window box.

"Flowers can grow anywhere. All they need is a fighting chance—a little sun, water, and somebody to look after them," Mom would say.

I almost picked one of those flowers on my way over to the racetrack. Then I realized it wouldn't be there anymore when I got back.

Rose of Sharon was entered in the seventh race, and I didn't want to spend any more time trapped inside that jockeys' room than I had to. So I started walking over from the dorms just a few minutes before the third race was supposed to be run.

Dag trained a horse in the third race, one that Rafael groomed.

When I got there, I could hear the track announcer's voice echoing through the grandstand. The field was already racing down the backstretch, heading into the far turn. Rafael was cheering for his horse by the finish line, with Nacho and Anibal on either side of him, cheering too.

That's when part of the crowd let out an *"OOOHH!"*

Dag's horse had broken down, dropping far behind the others until he slowed to a dead stop.

I heard a man cursing as he ripped up a thick stack of betting tickets.

"God damn it!" the man yelled, before tossing them into the air like confetti.

Rafael tugged hard at the empty lead he was holding from both ends, and I heard that leather strap pop between his hands.

The jockey had jumped off and was holding that injured horse by the bridle. Even with the rest of the runners roaring through the stretch, Rafael tried to jump the rail to get there. But Nacho and Anibal held him back until the race was over.

Then the three of them went sprinting up the homestretch toward Rafael's horse.

My heart told me to follow them, but my weight wouldn't shift. It was like my brain had talked my feet into believing they were nailed to the concrete. It had been one week since I left home, and now I wasn't sure who I was or what to feel.

Was that really supposed to be me, chasing after beaners on an Arkansas racetrack to help? Maybe Dad was somewhere right now chasing their kind through the streets with a stick.

I looked over at Dag, who hadn't moved a muscle except to get on his cell phone. That convinced me to hop the rail. And when my feet sank into that soft, damp earth, I swear they started running on their own.

By the time I got to Nacho and his brothers, a horse ambulance was already there.

Rafael had his arms wrapped around his horse's head.

"Eee-sy ba-by," he said with tears in his eyes. "No move. Eee-sy."

Both Anibal and Nacho had a hand on Rafael's shoulder.

The horse's right rear ankle was dangling from its leg, six inches off the ground, like a bag of crushed ice.

The racetrack vets put up a blue screen to hide that sight from the crowd.

"No can save?" Rafael asked the vets, without getting an answer.

Then one of the vets took a needle out of a black bag and gave that horse an injection.

I didn't know how much time the horse had left. But without Rafael there it probably wouldn't have been worth living.

Inside of a minute that injured horse had collapsed dead to the ground.

I looked at Rafael's face, and except for myself over the last five months, I'd never felt more sorry for anyone in my life.

The four of us walked back toward the finish line together without saying a word. We didn't have to. That empty lead strap slung over Rafael's shoulder said enough.

I turned back around at the sound of an engine and saw a tractor shoving that horse's lifeless body into the ambulance.

That picture stuck hard in the pit of my stomach.

"I'm sorry," somebody from the crowd told Dag, who just nodded his head politely.

Only, nothing had really touched *him*.

Chapter Eleven

I SIGNED INTO THE jockeys' room for the clerk and stepped onto the main scale. The needle behind the glass swung up slowly and then jerked back again, settling into one spot. I'd gained a whole pound from the day before and was up to 106. But I didn't feel like I had any more weight to me.

Then I passed through the swinging doors, heading toward my locker, when a rider named Samuel cut me off.

"My horse breaks from the starting gate right next to yours today, and I want you to know something," he said with breath that reeked like ammonia. "Don't get in my way on the track, or I'll hurt you. I got a family to support. I don't need to be looking over my shoulder for a bug who can't control a horse."

I stepped back, nearly gagging from his breath. I could almost see his tongue pushing through his paper-thin teeth.

"You see these fingers? I've broken every one," Samuel kept on, with his anger building and his voice getting louder. "Broke my right kneecap, ribs, elbows—both of them. And the point of *this* collarbone was sticking through the skin one time a quarter of an inch. That was a badge of honor no one else here could match. But I'm forty-three now, and these bones are too brittle to take much more. God forbid I get hurt because of you. God forbid!"

That's when a kid around my age, and nearly six inches taller, came through the doors waving a magazine.

"Pop, look at this new model XL with the blacked-out windows and titanium rims," he said, excited.

But Samuel blew, slapping him hard in the back of the head.

"What did I tell you about interrupting?" he ripped into the kid. "I'm talking business here. The business that puts food on the table for you."

The kid cowered away and said, "I'm sorry, Pop. I'm sorry."

I could almost feel myself standing in that kid's shoes.

Then Samuel turned back to me, but Parker rushed in between us, pushing me toward my locker.

"He'll keep clear of you on the track," Parker told Samuel in a soft voice, like he was trying to calm a crazy man. "Don't worry. You just go about your business now."

"What's eating him? And his breath?" I asked Parker at my locker.

"Yeah, 'eatin's' the right word," he answered low. "Just be thankful you're not *his* son. How many times I seen that boy get smacked for no reason, I can't count."

I raised my eyes to see Samuel still lecturing his son in the corner.

"Samuel's got trouble holding his food down. A few of the riders in here do. His emotions are tied up tighter than a knot from all the vomiting he has to do to make his riding weight," Parker said. "That's why his breath smells like that, from all the stomach acids that come up with his food. It eats away at the teeth, too. That's why they wanted to shove that submarine sandwich up your ass yesterday. Some of the jocks in here would kill to be able to eat like you and not pack on the pounds."

"Well, somebody should stop him from smacking his kid," I said.

"That's for the clerk or another jock or his own valet to do—not me, and especially not you. Truth is you're as far on the bottom 'round here as it gets," said Parker, shoving a white towel at me. "Now, go hit the steam room and drop that pound you picked up. You're listed to ride at a hundred and eight pounds today. You need to be three pounds lighter than that to make up for the saddle and things."

I stripped down to my shorts and headed for the steam room with that towel draped across my shoulders, covering the bruise I'd got from El Diablo. On the way I passed by Samuel and his son, who were looking at that car magazine together. The kid was smiling like everything was all right now. But I wondered how many cracks would have been showing if I could have seen his feelings on the inside.

I opened the door to the steam room, getting hit with a wave of heat that nearly knocked me flat. I stepped through the foggy steam and saw Gillette and Castro. They were both sitting there naked on the wooden benches, with their towels spread out beneath them.

"This room's for *men*, not bugs," said Gillette, chewing on ice chips from a plastic cup.

"That's right. You're not even man enough to lose those shorts," cackled Castro. "Probably needs to hide all his shortcomings."

So I took them off without saying a word and sat on my towel too.

"How'd you like that mud bath yesterday, bug?" asked Gillette, rattling his ice.

"Wasn't what I planned," I answered, with the sweat starting to pour out of me.

"Well, you better get used to it," said Castro. "From what I seen of your skills, you and the ground are gonna become good friends."

I was really starting to wilt in that heat when I saw the outline of Dad's face coming through a cloud of steam. Then the rest of his body came. He was sitting there naked, right next to them, with a bottle of whiskey in his hand.

Every part of me tensed up at the sight of him.

"So how much weight you need to lose, bug?" asked Castro.

"One pound," I answered in a shaky voice.

"Must be that *diet* catching up to you," said Gillette. "Not that you'll last at this game, but when you get a little older, you'll see how hard it is to keep the fat off—to keep that wolf from your door."

Then I heard Dad begin to howl at Gillette.

AAAAWWWOOOOOOO!

"But you'll never win a race. Not one that's run on the up-and-up," Gillette said. "You got 'loser' written all over you. It's probably in your genes."

Dad balled up a fist and pounded at his chest like Tarzan.

And I nearly jumped out of my skin at the sound of every thump.

"Gi-am-banco? I'll bet he comes from some trailer-park trash," said Castro. "The kind that hates Mexicans like me 'cause we outwork them."

Dad's face turned so angry, like he was ready to rip Castro a new one.

Then Dad smashed that bottle on the seat.

Castro was still talking. But his words were just a jumble to me as Dad stood up over him.

I dug my fingernails on both hands into the damp wood.

I'm not sure how it happened, but Dad must have turned all that anger inside himself, swallowing it whole, because I watched him turn the jagged edges of that bottle toward his own throat.

"Stop!" I screamed. "Stop it!"

"Hey! Lower your voice, kid!" demanded Gillette. "People will think we're puttin' a beatin' on you in here!"

I wiped the stinging sweat from my eyes, and suddenly Dad was gone. I didn't know where that scene had come from—probably my own mind. I just knew it shook me to see. And it felt so real I couldn't turn away or close my eyes to it, like a truth I had to accept.

Gillette and Castro wrapped towels around their waists, getting up to leave, as Parker's black face appeared in the door's glass window.

I followed right behind them—I wouldn't stay in there by myself for a second.

I was still shaking over that vision of Dad as Parker shined my riding boots and laid out my silks on a hanger. Dag didn't own Rose of Sharon. Someone else did. Their silks were white with a big red heart on the front that was almost the width of my chest.

I put on my protective vest and those silks, and I strapped on my riding helmet. Then I took the whip and cracked myself once in the chest and head just to prove I couldn't feel a thing and nothing could get to me.

That's when I heard somebody playing a horn from the other side of those swinging doors. I stepped through, and it was the track bugler, wearing his fancy red coat and black top hat.

"What do you want to hear, kid?" he asked. "I know a million songs."

"Anything pretty," I answered.

"Yeah, everybody likes pretty," he said. "You know this one?"

Then he pushed his lips together and played.

Right away my ear hooked into it, and the clerk of scales

started singing along—"Somewhere over the rainbow, way up high . . ."

I was smiling, and the bugler stopped in the middle to ask, "So, kid, you win a race yet?"

"No," I answered, hanging my head.

"First time you do, and they lead your horse into the winner's circle, I'll play that song for you," he said, before walking out the door to the racetrack.

I had that tune in my head, tapping the whip on my boots to it, as I entered the paddock to ride Rose of Sharon. Nacho was leading her around the walking ring, and I could see she wasn't pumped up like before her last race. She was back to being her easygoing self.

"This is Mr. and Mrs. Heidel," Dag said, introducing me to Rose of Sharon's owners.

They were probably both in their eighties, and the man wore glasses as thick as old-fashioned Coke bottles.

"Good luck, son," he said in a gravely voice. "Bring her back safe."

"I will," I answered. "I like your silks."

"We've been married fifty-five years," he said, pointing back and forth between his wife and himself. "That heart's a symbol of our love."

Then his wife called me "Gillette."

Dag just grinned as the man explained twice into her *good ear* that Gillette was riding another horse in the race.

"This filly might be on a down cycle," Dag said, pulling me off to the side. "Her last win was a tough one. So don't punish her too much with the whip if she comes up empty."

If that was true, I couldn't understand why he was running her back on just three days' rest. Horses usually race every two or three weeks. But I knew better than to ask.

"No red tag," said Nacho, leading Rose of Sharon and me out to the racetrack.

A red tag gets put on a horse's bridle after a race if they've been claimed. Then another groom takes the horse away to a new barn.

Dag had practically put a FOR SALE sign on Rose of Sharon by dropping her so low in price after a big win.

"Rafael lose one horse to God. No lose this one to money," said Nacho, turning us loose and crossing himself. "*No rojo hoy. Please.*"

The bugler snapped to attention, blowing his horn, as the field of fillies stepped onto the track.

Dut-dut-dut-da-da-dut-da-da-dut-dut-da.
Da-da-da-dut-dut-dut-da-da-dut-dut-da.

A crowd was lined up against the rail for the post parade, and the odds board had Rose of Sharon as the betting favorite at a little less than 2–1.

"My grandmother could win on this horse, kid. Don't screw it up!"

"I wouldn't bet counterfeit money on you, Giambanco!"

"That's what Dagget does. He puts some nobody on a good horse, so everyone's afraid to bet. Then he cleans up."

"Can you just stay in the saddle on this one, kid?"

I couldn't shut those voices out.

Every word cut right through me.

After that mud bath I took, I wasn't sure how much confidence I had in myself.

I warmed up Rose of Sharon. But she felt almost numb beneath me, and she barely wanted to pick up her feet.

"If that filly had a shot in hell of winning today, I'd be riding her. Not you," sneered Gillette, jogging his horse past mine.

In my heart I knew that Gillette was right.

Rose of Sharon and me were loaded into the starting gate, and Samuel was on the filly in the stall to my left.

"Just don't get in my way, bug," he said, with his teeth nearly moving inside his mouth.

The gates sprang open and Rose of Sharon shot out first.

We were in front for maybe three strides, and every ounce of blood inside me was pumping just as fast.

But that was all the speed she had to give.

Suddenly, she started to feel like a bicycle I'd put into eighteenth gear to climb some mountain of a hill. The other fillies went flying past her, and I could see the tail end of every one of them.

I shook the reins at her. Only, she was too tired to run.

We passed the spot where Rafael's horse had broken down and had to be destroyed. And I never even thought about raising the whip to her.

By the time we came off the turn into the homestretch, Rose of Sharon was so far behind, it probably looked like we were winning the race that started *after* this one.

But we made it past the wire, and I'd finished my first race in the saddle.

I jogged her back toward the grandstand to a chorus of boos and comments.

"You're garbage, Giambanco!"

"Dead last!"

That's when I lost my focus, and maybe something spooked her, but Rose of Sharon dumped me on my ass. Then she took off running through the stretch the wrong way, without me.

"The race is over, you idiot!"

I just remember somebody bringing Rose of Sharon back and fixing a red tag to her bridle.

Cap Daly had claimed her for $10,000.

Tammie led her off the racetrack, screaming at Dag, "You ruined her with your damn milk shakes. She's too sore to run."

Dag never lost his cool. Not even with me.

"You just brush off your pride, Gas. And make sure you're ready to ride Bad Boy Rising tomorrow," he said.

Before I got back to the jockeys' room, Parker intercepted me.

"This way, boss," he said, turning me down a long hall. "The stewards want to see you in their office."

The stewards are racing's referees.

There were three of them sitting around a big oak table, looking at me like I was a joke and a menace on the track.

"This is simple, Mr. Giambanco," one of them said, with Parker standing by my left shoulder. "You've had two rides and been on the ground twice. You get one more chance. If something goes wrong tomorrow, we'll suspend your license. And if I were you, I'd find a way to cover up the flames on those boots. El Diablo disgraced this sport, and you're not winning any sympathy points with us by wearing them."

Chapter Twelve

THAT NIGHT RAFAEL WAS near tears over losing his horse. Nacho and Anibal took him to the cantina, trying to cheer him up. There was nothing left in front of me except an empty dorm room, so I decided to tag along.

The place was packed tight with beaners, and both TVs were blaring the replays of the races at Pennington.

"*Qúe lástima,*" said Rafael, shaking his head. "*Era un caballo con mucho corazón.*"

"*Sí. Con mucho carazón,*" said Nacho, tapping his chest. "Much heart."

Anibal brought four opened bottles of beer to our table and slid one in front of me. I wrapped my fingers around the neck of the cold bottle, but I wouldn't take a sip.

Tammie walked through the front door and right over to

where we were sitting. She came up behind Rafael, dropping her hands on top of his shoulders like she could squeeze the sadness out of him.

"*Lo siento,*" she told him. "I'm so sorry."

Then she took the chair next to me, looking at the beer in my hand.

"*You* want to drink it?" I asked her.

"Not really. And it looks like you don't either," she said, seeing how much was left.

"Rose of Sharon. She o-kay?" asked Nacho.

"Her feet are sore. I had her standing in warm water and Epsom salts," Tammie answered, pointing to her own feet. "*Agua caliente.*"

Nacho lowered his eyes to his beer, like he was the worst groom in the world.

But everybody at that table knew it was really Dag's fault.

"Maybe my grandpa will let you ride her someday, after she gets healthy," Tammie told me.

"Yeah. If the stewards don't yank my license first," I said, feeling sorry for myself.

That's when El Diablo arrived. As he walked past us, El Diablo saw the tears in Rafael's eyes and said, "*Solamente un caballo*—just a horse, no a person. Be a man—*un hombre.*"

Rafael flew up from his chair, grabbing El Diablo around the collar with both hands, shoving him back a few feet.

I jumped up as fast as Nacho and Anibal to help, before El Diablo wiped the floor with him. But El Diablo never picked up his hands, or even tried to fight back.

"*Soy un hombre!*" Rafael hollered, with the rest of us trying to pull him away. "*Soy un hombre!*"

"*Sí, ahora,*" said El Diablo, nodding his head. "You acting like man now."

I heard those words from El Diablo's mouth, and something deep inside my chest hardened like a rock.

Everyone in the cantina had stopped to watch that scene, and for a moment there was nothing but the sound of the TVs in the background.

On both screens the horses were loading into the gate for the race that Rafael's horse had broken down in.

Rafael let go of El Diablo and watched as the field streaked down the straightaway. It was only for a split second that you could see his horse take a little hop-step, pulling himself up, as the camera followed the rest of the runners around the racetrack.

Then Rafael grabbed his beer from the table and left the cantina, with Nacho, Anibal, Tammie, and me following behind.

We had just made it down the steps when El Diablo came outside.

"*Era un caballo bueno,*" El Diablo said, raising a beer bottle before pouring some out onto the ground. "*Por el muerto.*"

"*Gracias,*" said Rafael, spilling some of his beer too.

I took the full bottle I was holding and lifted it high.

I poured every bit of it onto the ground and watched it seep in.

"For the dead," I said, hoping Mom would be riding Rafael's horse in heaven.

"*Sí. Por el muerto,*" echoed Nacho.

The next morning at the barn Dag didn't say a single word to me. But every time he passed by, I could see that toothpick rolling around in his mouth start to pick up speed.

"Could be special day for you today, bug," said Paolo, grinning wide. "Who knows, you might win your first race. Has to happen sometime."

I did nothing for hours but walk horses in circles. And every time I passed Bad Boy Rising's stall, his huge, fiery eyes seemed to zero in on mine.

Later on I saw the webbing up in front of Bad Boy's stall as the other horses were getting fed and he wasn't.

He was raising his voice about it too.

One of those sparrows nesting in the cracked wall of his stall was perched on the webbing, listening to him, until that sparrow finally spread its wings and flew off.

When I got to the jockeys' room, Parker had already covered up the flames on El Diablo's boots with black shoe polish.

"Maybe this will give you a brand-new start on things, boss," said Parker, showing me the boots. "Lord knows, you really need one."

"You're right," I said as the ceiling lights glistened off them.

Gillette and Castro were both in my race, and the two of them were already riding me hard.

"I hear this will be your last day in the saddle, bug," said Gillette.

"You mean his last day *out of the saddle*, don't you?" piped in Castro. "And that'll only be *funny* if nobody gets hurt but him."

Samuel was in the race too. But I didn't see him anywhere.

His son was sitting alone by Samuel's locker, and something made me walk over there.

"Don't matter what those guys say," he said, looking up at

me from his chair. "You're lucky. I wish I was small enough to ride."

"Why?" I asked him.

"My great-grandfather was a rider, my grandfather rode races, and now my father. I ruined it by being tall. I can't play basketball, and I'm scared to death of horses," he said, shifting a worried eye over to the bathroom door.

"I was scared of horses once," I said, looking at the faint outline of a bruise on his chin.

I could feel my own bruises, even the ones that had faded and disappeared. And I knew I needed to do something about them, so I headed for the bathroom.

It was empty inside, except for one stall with the door closed.

I could hear someone puking his guts up in there.

Then I heard a flush.

Samuel stepped out of that stall glaring at me, wiping his mouth with the back of his hand.

"Nobody likes to get smacked," I said. "Especially kids."

"Yeah? I'd slap you down right now, but I hear the stewards are getting ready to do that and boot you outta here," he sneered. "So why should I risk the fine?"

"I'm not going anywhere," I said. "I'm staying right here."

"Where? The can?" he said with a smirk, his voice echoing off the white tiled walls as he walked toward the door. "You just stay right *here*, bug. We all got a dump we need to take. Don't we?"

Chapter Thirteen

A HALF HOUR BEFORE I was supposed to ride Bad Boy Rising, the clerk of scales paged my name over the loudspeaker, "Gaston Giambanco Jr., report up front."

I passed through the swinging doors, and Dag was standing there.

He put an arm around me and walked me out of the jockeys' room into the hallway. I was already wearing his black silks with the coiled-up cobra on my chest. Then Dag settled us alone and out of sight behind a vending machine.

"This is for you, Gas," said Dag, handing me a betting ticket. "I plunked down fifty bucks to win on Bad Boy Rising for you. He's thirty-five to one right now. That's eighteen hundred you'll get back when he wins. But the odds are sure to go up before the race."

"So he's got a chance today?" I asked.

"He's got more than a *chance*," he answered. "Just make damn sure you hold on to him. That's all."

"If he's such a good thing, how come I'm riding?" I kept at Dag.

"Think there's any other reason you're in the saddle except that I'm looking for a big score?" he said low. "After the horses I've set you up on, and you falling off left and right, people wouldn't bet a dime on Gaston Giambanco Jr. if he was riding the only Thoroughbred in a pack of mules."

I felt like an idiot, and *smaller* than a bug. I couldn't stand the sight of myself in Dag's mirrored shades anymore, so I dropped my eyes down to El Diablo's boots with the covered-up flames.

"You don't look away when I'm talking," said Dag, slapping my face.

I could feel the fire start to rage inside me. I thought about tackling Dag on the spot. But I knew everything he held over me, like how old I really was, living in the dorms, and my job at his barn.

"Now, you just deliver for me today, Gas," he said in an easy voice, rubbing his fingers across my stinging cheek. "Because you'll really be delivering for yourself, too. *Comprende?*"

I nodded my head, thinking how Bad Boy Rising was probably milk-shaked to the top of his stomach.

Then Dag walked off, and I stuffed that betting ticket into one of my boots.

As I entered the paddock, Parker had just finished helping Dag saddle Bad Boy Rising. Then I watched Dag check the saddle twice, making sure it was tight enough not to slip.

Parker started back in my direction.

"Moment of truth, boss," Parker said, walking past. "Just hang on to what you really want."

Bad Boy was so pumped up that he couldn't keep still. His eyes were wild and his nostrils flared. Then he began bucking like he'd just been fed an entire case of Jolt cola.

Nacho already had him on the walking ring, but nothing outside of racing three quarters of a mile on the dead run was going to burn off what was churning inside of Bad Boy.

Paolo was bouncing around too, probably waiting to cash in on his bets. Only Dag was playing it cool on the surface.

"Riders up!" called an official.

Dag never shook my hand for good luck. But the last thing I felt before I climbed aboard Bad Boy Rising was Dag's cold-blooded grip on my leg, hoisting me into the saddle.

Nacho was shaking almost as much as Bad Boy.

"This no good, Gas," said Nacho as we got out of Dag's earshot. "My family no treat horses this way. *Es muy malo.*"

As we headed for the racetrack, I saw Tammie outside of the paddock fence looking in. I knew she could read the signs all over Bad Boy Rising.

Tammie shook her head at me one time before she turned away, and I couldn't remember when I'd felt more ashamed.

Then Nacho turned us loose on the track, and I was left to wrestle with Bad Boy Rising on my own.

I saw we were 73–1 on the odds board now.

I thought about that ticket Dag gave me. How it was burning a hole in my boot. I couldn't even begin to multiply seventy-three times fifty. But I knew that kind of money would solve lots of problems for me.

I couldn't control Bad Boy in the post parade past the grandstand, and he just galloped off ahead of the other horses.

But I heard every catcall from those bettors.

"It's ten to one that you can even stay in the saddle, Giambanco."

"Ten? I'll give you twenty to one this bug don't make it out of the gate."

I wanted to show them all. I wanted to win by the length

of the stretch and send them all home broke while I filled my own pockets.

Only, I knew that would make me the same as Dag.

We reached the starting gate, and Bad Boy Rising was so hyped up the assistant starters couldn't get him inside of it. Finally two of them stood on either side of him, locking their arms together behind his rear end.

Then they tried to bum-rush Bad Boy into the gate.

But Bad Boy reared up on his hind legs.

He went up so high I had to jump off his back, afraid he'd flip over.

"Stay there. That's where you belong, bug," cracked Samuel as I picked myself up off my ass.

"It's his home away from home," laughed Gillette.

All the other horses went in without a problem, and everyone was waiting on us. I kept my feet planted on the ground until the assistant starters won their tug-of-war with Bad Boy and got him into the gate.

An ambulance pulled up, ready to follow behind the field.

I looked just over the inside rail and saw a single yellow rose growing on a bush there. It was stretching toward the sky, with its petals opened wide, shining in the sunlight.

And right then I remembered the best part of who I was.

I was Gaston Giambanco Jr., with a name that sounded like music if you said it right. The way Mom did.

So I kissed the tattoo with Mom's name on it, right through Dag's silks. Then I climbed that iron monster and got back into the saddle on Bad Boy Rising.

The sound of a bell split the air and the metal doors sprang open. Suddenly, I felt like I was on a rocket sled instead of a racehorse. Bad Boy exploded to the lead, and only a sparrow flying off my shoulder for the first forty yards was ever close to him.

The wind was rushing at me so fast I had to clench my teeth closed to stop the breath from being sucked out of my lungs.

There were nine other Thoroughbreds strung out behind us as I shifted my weight left, leaning into the turn.

I was holding on for my life more than I was riding.

I could feel every muscle in Bad Boy's body twitching, and I would have believed he was hooked up to a car battery. And even if some other horse did try to run us down from behind, Bad Boy Rising was so juiced up on that illegal junk he'd probably savage him, tearing into that horse's throat with his teeth.

We straightened away into the homestretch at nearly forty miles per hour, and I could hear the track announcer's echoing voice: "They've all got Bad Boy Rising to catch at big odds!"

I shot past the grandstand in front by five lengths, and I knew those big-mouth bettors would be choking on their words now.

But in my mind I could hear Gillette saying how I'd never win a race, not unless somebody handed it to me.

I remembered the smack Dad gave that horse on the behind before it ran off and dumped me. And I could almost feel the sting of Dag's slap across my face again.

So I squeezed the whip tight inside my right hand. Out of pure anger I raised that whip up, ready to crack Bad Boy Rising a good one for no reason except maybe to feel better about myself.

But something from deep inside me fought that feeling back, pulling the whip down just as quick.

An eighth of a mile from the wire I peeked over my shoulder.

No horse was getting any closer.

In fast-forward I could see Mom smiling as she galloped a horse along a trail, the shame in Nacho's eyes, and Tammie turning away from me in disgust at the paddock fence.

I took a deep breath, and then seventy yards from the finish line I jumped.

Bad Boy Rising went scorching down the track without me.

For a second I swore I'd sprouted wings.

Then the ground came rushing up fast, hitting me hard in the mouth. A sharp pain shot through my neck and shoulders as I skidded to a stop, with my face plowed into the dirt. On my arm I could feel the tattoo of the cross with my mother's name burning.

I heard the hooves of the other horses rumbling toward me, like an earthquake about to hit. I couldn't tell the trembling of the ground from my own.

I felt the first hoof hit my helmet. And as I went rolling, the next slammed me in the chest, shaking me to the core.

After that I must have blacked out.

Chapter Fourteen

I OPENED MY EYES in the ambulance. I was wearing a clear oxygen mask over my nose and mouth, and the sound of a siren was screaming through my brain.

Nacho was there with me, squeezing my hand and praying in Spanish.

Looking up at him, I'd noticed for the first time that his eyes were the exact same shade of brown as Mom's.

The next time I regained consciousness was in the hospital.

It was just doctors and nurses around me. I guessed they'd pumped me full of drugs, because I wasn't feeling any pain. And when I shut my eyes, I felt like I'd just jumped from Bad Boy's back and was still flying.

When my head finally cleared, I felt Tammie's lips go flush against mine.

"You're going to be all right, Gas," she said, with her eyes full of tears.

I had to focus hard to figure out if that kiss was real or part of some dream. Cap was there with her. So were Nacho, Rafael, and Anibal.

I was dressed in a blue hospital gown, with my right arm in a sling and a wide bandage wrapped so tight around my chest and ribs that I could barely breathe.

"The protective vest you wore most likely saved your life," said the doctor on duty. "A hoof hit you directly over the heart. Without that protection it probably would have penetrated into the chest cavity. As it is, you suffered a bruised heart, some cracked ribs, and a broken collarbone. You're a very lucky young man."

The EMS workers had cut Dag's silks off of me when I got brought in, but on the nightstand to my left were El Diablo's boots, with the flames beginning to peek through the black polish.

"Why'd you do it, Gas?" asked Cap. "Why'd you jump?"

"I couldn't win that way," I answered. "Not like that."

That's when Tammie pulled the fifty-dollar win ticket from her pocket.

"The doctors told us this was inside your boot," said Tammie, crumpling the ticket in a fist.

"Dag bet it for me," I said. "With whatever money he put on Bad Boy for himself."

"Well, Bad Boy Rising crossed the finish line first," said Tammie. "It's too bad for Dag the racetrack doesn't pay off on a horse that finishes without a jockey on its back."

"How's Bad Boy?" I asked.

"Good. Still mean. Thinks he won race," said Nacho.

Dag never showed his face at the hospital, or even called once to see how I was. But that first night, way past visiting hours, I looked up and El Diablo was standing in the doorway.

"I see you earn your badge of honor," he said, pointing to my collarbone as he stepped inside.

I started to explain why I'd jumped. But El Diablo broke in and said, "No matter what anybody say. No matter what stewards do. You're a winner. No one ever call you bug again in front of me."

Then he reached over to the nightstand and picked up one of the boots. His eyes ran up and down it like he was looking for something lost.

"I know you'll be needing those back," I said.

"No more borrow," he said, scratching away some of the black polish with a fingernail. "Boots yours to keep."

"Why?" I asked. "Nobody's ever gonna let me ride again."

"Not important now," El Diablo answered. "They needed clean start. That you already give."

By the middle of the next day, Tammie told me, all the TV stations had played the video clip of me jumping, and there were pictures of it in all the newspapers, too.

The stewards pulled my jockey's license and ordered that Bad Boy Rising's urine be tested.

"Yeah, but the only way they can prove a milk shake is to test for carbon dioxide. The one test they don't give here," Tammie said in a frustrated voice. "So Dag's gonna come off smelling like a rose."

Cap and the police got to the hospital at about the same time that afternoon. And I saw that one of those officers was wearing a Texas Lone Star badge.

They talked in the hallway for a while with Cap.

I figured that Dad had seen me on TV and I was about to get nailed for being a runaway.

But Cap came into my room alone with a sad look on his face.

"Gas, I've got some bad news for you," he said, removing his Kangol. "Your father's passed away. They say he's been gone about a week. Neighbors found him in the house a few days ago."

For a minute or two I sat up in bed, stunned. I guess my brain was busy searching my feelings from top to bottom.

Then all at once the tears came.

I loved Dad, and losing him shook me hard.

But I started thinking about another side of it too.

Dad had drunk himself to death, almost like he wanted to. And maybe he was finally going to find some peace.

I didn't think about the times he hit me, or everything he'd taught me about how "beaners" were ruining our lives.

Instead, I remembered him leading those two big horses around the riding stable, with them acting like they loved him to death. And how happy it made Mom to ride again.

Then I wondered how long he'd been watching Nacho and his brothers look after me, and if Dad had learned as much as I did.

Epilogue

AFTER FOUR DAYS I left the hospital, and the Texas Department of Family and Protective Services placed me in a foster home about a mile from my old high school so I could get ready to start my senior year.

It didn't matter to Tammie that I'd lied about my age, or anything else.

"You had every reason to hide the truth," she said before I left. "Besides, Grandpa taught me never to put too much stock in what people say. He taught me to watch what they do. And I don't have any complaints from what I've seen in you."

That's when *I* kissed *her*, and she didn't back off a step.

Nacho brought my clothes over to the hospital from the dorm, and I let him keep my yellow ID from the racetrack.

"You see him," I said, pointing to the Polaroid of me on it. "No brothers when he came here. Now maybe three—Rafael, Anibal, and Ignacio."

"*Todos hijos de María,*" he said as we clasped hands.

That next month Cap wrote Child Protective Services a letter asking for a custody hearing. Tammie was back at college by then. But Cap drove down to Texas and even put on a suit and tie for me.

"The way I see it, the only family Gas has now works at Pennington Racetrack in Arkansas," Cap said at the hearing. "If you see fit to let him come live with me, I'll see that he finishes high school, makes his own mind up about college, and learns a trade that he loves—grooming and caring for horses. But not as a jockey. At least, not yet."

Maybe the family court judge saw what I'd seen in Cap's eyes, a steadiness that said he wasn't going to move off the spot he was standing on. And that he'd be standing in the same place for *me* tomorrow.

"What do you say about that idea, Gaston?" the judge asked.

"I think that's where I belong," I answered, without having to think.

Within a few weeks it all got worked out, after my

caseworker agreed to make the trip to Pennington every month to check up on me.

Before I left Texas, I visited Mom's grave.

There was still no headstone. That was something I wanted for her and was willing to work and save money to buy.

I wanted everyone who passed to know how special she was.

So I picked a bunch of wildflowers that day and left them with her for safekeeping.

Dad was buried on the other side of the hill, and I went there next.

I realized that any headstone for him would have my name on it too:

GASTON GIAMBANCO

But I knew I was a lot luckier than he was.

I'd sidestepped most of the anger that had turned him inside out. And I swore right then that if I ever had a son, I'd never lay a hand on him.

I still think about that illegal and what he did to get Mom killed. I can't completely escape that. But I don't let those feelings for him, wherever he is, rule my life anymore and make me into somebody I don't want to be.

Going back to Arkansas meant I'd have to see Dag again.

But after everything that had happened with me and Bad Boy Rising, Pennington Racetrack started testing for carbon dioxide to stop horses from being milk-shaked. And a week before I got there, Dag moved his entire stable to a track in Oklahoma that didn't test for it.

That meant that Ignacio and his brothers lost their jobs.

So did El Diablo.

Cap did what he could to give them all some work, after he'd picked up a few more horses to train. But within a month Ignacio and his brothers moved to California to groom horses with their father. And they planned on sending for their mother to join them soon.

"It better together—whole family, one place," Ignacio told me the day he and his brothers got on the bus.

I nodded my head and said, "*Sí*. You're right."

I talk to Tammie a couple of times a week on the phone. She always asks about the horses, especially Rose of Sharon. I don't know what's going to happen between Tammie and me. I just know that I want her in my life.

Every morning before school I go with Cap to the barn, learning all I can about horses.

I still walk Rose of Sharon in the courtyard under that shade tree. And sometimes I stop beneath its outstretched branches, planting my feet down into the fresh earth as far as they'll go.